THE BIG DREAM

REBECCA ROSENBLUM

THE BIG DREAM

STORIES

BIBLIOASIS

FIRST EDITION

Library and Archives Canada Cataloguing in Publication

Rosenblum, Rebecca, 1978-
    The big dream : stories / Rebecca Rosenblum.

ISBN 978-1-926845-28-9

    I. Title.

PS8635.O65B55 2011   C813'.6   C2011-903446-8

  Canada Council   Conseil des Arts
for the Arts   du Canada

 Canadian   Patrimoine
Heritage   canadien

ONTARIO ARTS COUNCIL
CONSEIL DES ARTS DE L'ONTARIO

Biblioasis acknowledges the ongoing financial support of the Government of Canada through The Canada Council for the Arts, Canadian Heritage, the Canada Book Fund; and the Government of Ontario through the Ontario Arts Council.

   BIO GAZ

PRINTED AND BOUND IN CANADA

For
Carl & Hilda Rubin
and
Herschel & Sonya Rosenblum
My Grandparents

CONTENTS

Dream Big / 9

Waiting for Women / 23

Complimentary Yoga / 39

The Anonymous Party / 55

After the Meeting / 69

Bursting into Tears Every Twenty Minutes / 77

Cheese-Eaters / 87

How to Keep Your Day Job / 101

Sweet / 111

Research / 127

Loneliness / 143

Dream Inc. / 155

This Weather I'm Under / 173

DREAM BIG

THE CAFETERIA WAS CLOSED for renovations and the temporary lunchroom was in the basement. In fact, the temporary lunchroom was actually a meeting room with tables, folding chairs, a microwave, four vending machines, and no windows. Many employees chose to eat at their desks, but some made use of the room.

Clint peeled the plastic off his Crackerz'n'cheze.

"*Cheze* does not look like an English word." said Anna. She was eating unstirred fruit-at-the-bottom yoghurt.

"Still delicious." Luddock was eating a mustard-soaked sandwich. The sheer yellow bread revealed the pink of bologna.

"Of course." Anna reached the fruit layer and beamed into her plastic cup.

"Listen – " Clint leaned forward "Remember, last Tuesday – ?"

"No!" Luddock waved his sandwich. Bread flapped away from meat. "I download all previous-week memories to the main server at midnight on Saturdays. Frees up disc space for current work."

"Luddock, no!" Anna squawked, mouth full of pureed berries. "This is not a Tech Support situation. Do not make Tech jokes."

"Actually, only Tech is sitting at this table."

"Lunch is our own time. We could be sitting with another department, people who don't even work here. We shouldn't make this a closed conversation."

"Anna-cat, *how* would we eat lunch with people who don't work here? Unless we walked to the airport?"

Anna set down her empty berry yoghurt and opened the peach. "We might someday end up in a central location, freed from the horrid lunchroom – "

"Well, it isn't *hor*rid . . ." said Clint. Some cheese residue stuck to the package, eluding the spreader. Clint thought about Virgie safe in her lab, unavailable for judgment, then licked the plastic.

"It's not impossible that we might someday work near a mall with a food court."

"Dream big." Luddock sealed his empty Tupperware. "That was very anticlimactic, Anna. Not at all worth quashing my server joke. What were we talking about?"

Clint's Crackerz'n'cheze were just supposed to be the appetizer, but the margarine container of tuna casserole was no longer in his lunch sack. The mysteries of the office fridge. "Tuesday, last Tuesday, my three-month anniversary cake."

Luddock nodded. "I vaguely recall. Sure was nice of us."

Anna was eating fast, already down to the peach layer. "A joyous day. You're no longer fireable without just cause *and* you can finally go to the dentist."

"Dentist, orthopedist, psychiatrist, all your problems are solved now, Clinty. Plus cake." Luddock was flicking bits of napkin at the finance team. They hadn't noticed.

"No one else remembered."

"I hate to say it, but not everyone loves you as much as we do, Clinty."

Clint thought of Virgie's kiss at his door, her hand on his cheek. "No, but, like, management. Mai-Nam didn't give me a full-time offer. My contract ended last week. Technically, I don't work here right now."

"Oh, but you do." Anna's curls tossed. "We've got to do that image file migration, and the emphasis is on *we*, buddy."

"C'mon, Luddock, spitballs?"

Anna flicked one. "They don't actually contain spit. They are actually quite dry."

"Ok, like, if I'm a real employee, *like I was promised,* shouldn't I have signed a benefits agreement by now?"

Anna nodded. "Did you hear from HR?"

"No, or I wouldn't be asking you. I'd ask them." Clint had only had half a granola bar for breakfast. He'd given the other half to Anna on the bus.

Luddock was wadding a pear core, yoghurt cups, and snack-pack into a ball. Things were snapping and dripping out of his hands. Anna stood and pulled her skirt neatly over her knees. Clint stood too.

"You can't fight the power, man. All you can do is subvert." Luddock smashed everything into the wastebasket and clapped Clint's back with his sticky hand, pulling him away from the M&M machine into the hall.

"People with the kind of OSAP payments I got don't subvert."

"Good point. Before papers have been signed, industrial sabotage is risky."

"Be fun to set everyone's homepage to porn with sound, though."

"Hey, *I* might. *I'm* a salary-man. *You* just play the course for now."

Clint wondered if Anna was glaring because he'd mentioned porn. They went up the elevator, down the hall to the Tech cubes and the long hungry slope of afternoon.

*

Three weeks passed. Clint started keeping granola bars at his desk, but then a mouse gnawed through a Quaker Chewy Chocolate wrapper, and he switched to canned foods. He kept submitting time sheets and getting paid his probationary hourly wage. He helped Anna finish the art migration and started some menus for the invoice database. He made a PowerPoint about voicemail options. He played the course.

Clint didn't like to sleep at Virgie's during the week because it was so far from work, and he never remembered to bring all the right clothes. When he'd stay, she'd cook something good and didn't put on a T-shirt to sleep, but Mai-Nam had called him "semi-unprofessional" when Virgie's streetcar made him 37 minutes late, wearing sneakers.

The day he wore Virgie's socks (just black cotton, but they *felt* girlish) Clint noticed an ache at the back of his jaw.

"My mouth hurts," he said to Anna as she approached with their coffees.

"So you don't want this?" She pulled both cups to her chest, a coffee bra.

"I want it." He reached towards her breasts. "I'm just telling you."

"Why does it hurt? Are you stressed and grinding your teeth at night?"

"Dunno." The first sip scalded him above the molars. "My gums are sensitive."

"You didn't just say that." This was Luddock, from his cube. Luddock had a voice that didn't stop at baffles. "You sound 93 and constipated."

"I think that's an unrelated condition."

"Feel better, Clinty." Anna smiled at him with her strong, dairy-white teeth.

He did not feel better that day nor the next, and the morning after that, he woke with the whole right side of his mouth a dull tight throb.

"Ohhaahhh . . ." He meant to sigh, but it came out more of a groan. "Oh . . ."

"What," said Virgie, from far under the duvet.

"Nothing," said Clint, but it came out *Nawherm.* He tried again, "Nawtherm."

Virgie's frazzled braids appeared, her pale half-open grey eyes. "Are you dying?"

"Nah, nah." That sounded about right. "Too-ack."

"Toothache?" Her eyes blinked wider, but he knew she couldn't really see him without her glasses. "People don't actually get those. Not like headaches, come and go, meaningless. When your tooth hurts, something is *wrong* with your tooth. Which tooth?"

She was right in his face, trying to see in his mouth.

"Em fine."

She reached behind him for her wire rims on the bed stand. Her breasts swung against his chest.

"Open."

Clint opened his mouth like a baby bird.

"Oh, not good. It's all red and puffy – " Virgie actually poked in a finger, which tasted salty " – there in the back. Wisdom tooth. You need to see a dentist."

"Er." That should've been *no*, which should've been, *no money*. He made the slippery-fingered money sign.

She rubbed his cheek. "You're in pain, you need a professional to make it stop." Virgie had the innocence of youth, though they were the same age; staying in school let her stay naïve. She had a dental plan through the university. Her parents sent her birthday gifts of cash and flowers. Virgie had no idea about anything, including that Clint was broke or even could be.

*

The hot shower spray on his jaw softened the pain, but Clint still couldn't really chew his bagel. The first bite he just sucked until it dissolved, which took forever. Then he tried sucking bites with a mouthful of coffee, which was faster, but not very much.

"You're late," said Anna from under her desk. She emerged ass-first, hauling her power bar, skirt tucked between thighs. "Mai-Nam came by twice and both times I told her you were in the bathroom. Now she thinks there's something wrong with you."

"There *isth* thomething wrong."

"Are you gay now?"

"What?" Clint flopped into his chair, which rolled back and almost dumped him.

"Gay? You're lisping."

"I thin that's homahphobic, Anna," Clint said very carefully.

"You're probably right." She stood and shook out her skirt. "I'm sorry."

"Doan apologize to *me,* it's ther *gay* piple that – "

"Why are you *talking* like that, Clinty?"

"Toothache, still. Is all swollen."

"Ah, Jesus." Anna shook the electrical cord at the sky. "What next?"

Luddock strode in, shoelaces flapping. "Anna-cat, we're too busy to go on strike. Plug that in right now."

"Some wingnut on the third floor broke his. Mai-Nam said – "

"To render your own computer useless? What's wrong with – "

"Whuh? Hah do you *break* . . . ?"

"What, Clint, are you drunk?"

"The storeroom door is jammed. He stepped on it. Clint has a toothache. God, this place would fall apart without me." Anna left, swinging her cord like a lasso.

"*Tooth*ache? Oh, fuck, be a man, get some Ambersol . . . ." Luddock stomped out and then Clint could hear him trying to un-jam the storage-room door by kicking it.

*

Clint waited in the hallway outside Mai-Nam's office. It wasn't a real office – just a cube with a cardboard panel for a door. Clint could hear Mai-Nam's phone call perfectly: "Uh-huh, no, well, no, ok, Samsonite,*" click.* He tapped the panel gently. It sounded like thunder in a school play.

"Yo?"

"Hey, ah, Mai-Nam?" Clint slid inside and her small form popped up behind the two monitors, mounds of cables, Blackberry

and cell charging on top of stacks of papers on top of hardware car-
tons, on top of desk. There was a deflated McDonald's sack on her
ergonomic keyboard. Mai-Nam had a car and could go to McDonald's. She was staring at her monitor, scrolling rapidly.

"Hey, um, Clint. You know they got mice on the third floor?"

Clint enunciated carefully, "We got mies on this floor."

"Yeah, but are they eating the phone cords?"

"Er, nah yet." Clint tried to close the sliding panel but it
jammed.

"Well, they are on third. You'd think mice would be a maintenance problem, but anything telecommunications-related is an us
problem."

"Uh. Ye-ah." The door ripped. Most of it closed, but a corner
caught on a motherboard, leaving a lightning-bolt-shaped hole.
Clint saw high heels in the hall.

"So, I'm gonna send you and Anna down with the new cords –
in the cupboard, Luddock fixed the door – and these thingies."
Mai-Nam was waggling little metallic things on her fingers. They
looked like Clint's 9th grade retainer, only smaller. "They clip
cords under desks, see. But first you gotta glue'em on. Do you
know where any glue is?"

"Ah, no."

"I'll call Anna . . ." Mai-Nam reached for the phone.

"Lissen, I wanta talk to ya, about my – "

"Hmm? Listening . . ." Mai-Nam was in fact dialing, but not
the last digit.

" – contrad."

Mai-Nam put down the phone. "Yes, Clint? Yes?"

"Iss over. Three weks ago."

"Oh. *Oh.*" It seemed several of the clips were stuck on her
fingertips. Mai-Nam was yanking hard as she smiled at Clint.
"Don't worry, you'll still get paid for any hours you work, even
without a contract."

"Until?"

"Until . . ." She managed to tug off one of the clips, but the tug flung it across the room and out the hole in the door. "What?"

"I unnrerstood, I was given to unner*stand* . . . after the contrad, I'd be full-time."

"Well, that's the, uh, goal." Mai-Nam was squinting at her door. Clint stepped in front of the hole. "But we would have to request budget for another full-timer, get approval from HR, the allocations committee. This would take time."

Clint thought about the conditional voice, indicative of a thing that not only hadn't happened yet, but also might never. Clearly, not tomorrow. He wondered if he could get the allocations committee to feel the lump in his upper-right gums.

"Do I have to go thruh a review? To see if you want . . ."

Mai-Nam leapt up, feet catching a cord. Her laptop tipped back onto the screen. "Absolutely! It'll be time for your three-month review in a few . . ."

"Three weks ago," Clint said. He remembered suddenly the Cheez-its he'd left in his coat pocket, and the mouse. Mice. "If ya do der three-month review when der person's been here . . . three months."

"There*abouts*. I mean, that's the ideal but . . ." Mai-Nam started flipping papers off the desk. Her Blackberry skittered to the floor. She still had a retainer clipped to her thumb. The phone rang and she hit the speaker button without stopping her search.

A squawk: "Mai, if you don't get someone on these *fuck*ing cords, I'm gonna go ape-shit down here. Nothing's bleeding working, I'm on my *cell* . . . ."

Mai-Nam lifted a stack of what looked to be blank paper. The desk lamp that had been resting on it crashed to the floor. From the speaker: "What the *fuck*?"

Mai-Nam looked at Clint, the left corner of her mouth twitching like a cat's tail. "Could you just – just take those clips to Anna? She knows where the cords are? I just – this has to be done. I'll start on your . . ." her gaze drifted to the torn door ". . . stuff."

*

Virgie was disgusted and adorable, chopping carrots while wearing only a pink T-shirt and orange panties. "What a horrible manager. You should report her to HR."

"Tha's not really . . ."

"They take advantage. You work hard." Carrots into the steamer. Then peppers.

"Yes. And yes. But they won't – "

"They have to, they promised. Listen, can you eat *any*thing that isn't steamed? It's my folks' barbeque on Saturday, remember? My mom won't want to purée stuff."

"Virgie – " He had forgotten, or not forgotten, just not wanted to discuss. On Saturday, Tech was installing CallPilot on every phone in the office, not barbequing with Virgie's parents. "I cen't. Gotta work."

"What? No."

"Iss a big project, everbody's gotta."

"Overtime is optional." She waved the knife absently. "Real life is not optional."

It was sweet of her to think this. Sweet and delusional. "Virgie, werk *is* real life. I'm nah in a good spot rie now. Sometimes, they jus say, *come* and you gotta come."

"What about me? Can I just say, *come*?" She smiled, jutted her left hip towards him. He looked at the pale curve, the bright cotton. He was wasting a perfectly good girlfriend.

"I cen't do it, Virgie. Um sorry."

The smile dropped like a comet. "Yeah. Yeah, you are."

*

The mouse-proofing took Tech two days. First, they made every employee leave his or her desk for several minutes so that the clips could be glued on. Again the next day, when the glue was dry, so their phone wires could be locked into the clips. People were furious at the inconvenience, the violation of strangers crawling under their desks. Curses were thrown, and Damien actually got kicked.

On the third day, it was found that though cords were no longer resting on the floor, the jacks were low enough to be vulnerable to vermin. Tech was sent to cover the breach with wide rolls of packing tape. Anna muttered, "This spells disaster as soon as they reconfigure the furniture. That's gonna be a hell of a lot of sticky jacks."

Clint could have made several good dirty jokes out of that, but by then he wasn't really speaking unnecessarily.

Tech spent the morning wandering with their tape, wincing when they met, whispering, "We are universally loathed." This time, many people chose to remain at their desks while Clint huddled beneath, taping.

No mice were seen.

When the team reconvened in the Tech hallway, Mai-Nam was being fired. The woman firing her was tall, blonde, and never before seen in Tech. As Mai-Nam wept and threw things into boxes, the woman introduced herself as the VP of Human Resources. She offered them all time-and-a-half to finish taping cords that evening, when it would be "less of a disruption."

Damien was on server duty, icing his shin, and Lionel turned out to be a father and needed to get home, so it was only Anna, Clint, and Luddock who, in dread and faint slumber-party excitement, took scavenged food down to the basement for what Anna declared, "Lunch, the sequel!"

Clint carefully worked his work can opener around the tin of Spaghetti-Os, then stood. The turgid lump at the back of his mouth seemed to pulse. He went several steps towards the microwave before Luddock caught him in a flying tackle.

"Metal in the microwave equals death, Clint! You might be willing to sacrifice yourself, but the whole building radioactive for ten thousand years for warm noodles? No! No, I say."

Clint sat slowly, clutching the tin. "Cen't believe I forgot that."

Luddock flapped his hands. "It *is* tiresome, feeding oneself."

"That food-court fantasy gets fonder every day." Anna was eating a jam sandwich. It wasn't a real sandwich, just bread with red. "Oh, for a Cultures right now."

Clint took a forkful of Os. Warm, they could be mushed with the tongue, but otherwise they congealed almost solid. He sucked hard.

"The *best* is KFC on Toonie Tuesdays," said Luddock. "Sometimes, if you're charming, they'll give you two thighs instead of the thigh and drumstick classic."

Clint liked the Italian place, Mrs. Something, where you could get pizza with a side of lasagna. But noodles weren't dissolving, so he just nodded. KFC wasn't bad.

"The food court is democracy in action." Luddock flapped his arms. "Everything is an option."

Anna mentioned Mmmuffins, Kernels, the soup place. Luddock parried Manchu Wok, Teriyaki Experience, Mr. Greek Junior. It was a dreamy hour.

If there had been windows, they would have gone dark by the time the VP came down to declare the building empty enough that they could work. "I appreciate this, team. I really do." She clasped the nearest shoulder, Luddock's, who flinched.

In the fluorescent-lit night, the building was dead silent except the shriek of adhesive pulling free, the rustle of file-drawers searched for candy, control-top pantyhose, condoms. ("They're going to say we did *anyway* – why not learn something?")

Clint had dense regrets about the few Spaghetti-Os he'd managed to swallow. Crawling was not a fast or jerky enough activity to be nauseating, *one would think,* yet he could feel the sweet red sauce creeping up his throat as he hunched low, taped, shuffled backwards. He kept tonguing his gum-lump, though he knew he did not want to release the energy pent up there. Violent energy, the thrum of his heart in his gum line.

"The *thing* about Freshii," Luddock yelled from behind a rolling chair, "is that the *basic* salad costs six bucks, and then more for every little freaking walnut."

Clint began the labourious crawl across the aisle.

Behind him, Anna was crawling in the opposite direction. "Freshii is for the food courts of the upwardly mobile. They care not for the cost of nuts. They have spent $17 in gas driving their $45,000 cars to the mall anyway."

Forty-five thousand was slightly less than what Clint owed OSAP.

Luddock stood and started towards a foursome cube. While he was stepping over Anna's pink-bloused back, he said, "That'll be you, Anna-cat. Soon you'll be mobilizing upward, Tech supervisor, eatin' walnuts." He walked into the quad.

Anna sat back on her haunches. "What?"

"You've always run this joint, now you'll get the paper door to prove it."

Clint couldn't stand being on all fours any longer, face hanging down, the slosh of pus above his jawbone. He collapsed onto his right hip and then flopped back to stare at the ceiling. He wondered if Mai-Nam had much student debt, a boyfriend, a life.

"You think I'm gonna be Tech sup?"

"You're smart, nice, you don't cry in public." A shriek of tape. "Gotta be you."

Clint stared at a white tube of fluorescence. His vision was beginning to spot.

"Could be you. You're smart and unteary. Not so nice, but you can reach high shelves."

"Ah, but you're the chick. Tech sup's gotta be a chick."

"Really?"

"How else would you explain Mai-Nam? This time it so happens that the best man for the job is a woman, but that's just a bonus."

"The facts that I deserve the job and will get it are unrelated?"

"I think this is correct."

"I think this is the twenty-first century and you are incorrect."

A sigh, then Luddock's voice: "You with us, Clinty?"

"Umnaha."

"Yeah, well, the important thing, Anna-cat, is that *one* of us gets promoted soon, so that the full-time spot can slide over to our man on his back here before we lose him."

Clint was tonguing it again. He couldn't help it. It was like a sun radiating warmth all over his face. He realized suddenly he'd been supposed to meet Virgie at the movies.

"We go to the ER after this, yeah?" Anna again. "They'll have to treat him at least a little, right? Must've gone septic by now, and that's medical not dental."

"Hope so. We'll have to MapQuest the Mississauga hospital, I don't know it."

"It's gotta be on transit, it's a hospital. How many more rows?"

Clint was wondering if Virgie would've packed his few things yet, if she would've washed his socks and underwear or just packed them dirty.

"Four more rows. Canya hang on another hour, Clint?"

"Uma. Sure."

"Great. And it doesn't *gotta* be on transit, Luddock – Mississauga's fucked. But for Clint, we can get the cab."

"Hey, one of us is management now, of course we can." A breeze brushed his closed eyes, then another: they were walking over him. "Another hour until the hospital, Clinty. And in a few weeks, we'll get you all the insurance you need to get the thing just yanked right out of your skull. Hang in there."

Her words were as soft as the kicked-up air over his face, as melodious as a lullaby. Clint didn't mind the pain, or his underground apartment with no Virigie to visit. He didn't hear the hum of the fluorescent lights, the rush of traffic, the rustle of mice in the wall. Clint felt only the relief of fluid bursting against the roof of his mouth.

WAITING FOR WOMEN

WHEN NEITHER WOMAN had arrived by 6:12, Theo took the kids outside to wait. Jake put on his Transformers hat, scrambled off the porch and hurled his small denim body into the hedge, the glossy leaves closing behind him. Theo didn't know what was of interest in the hedge, nor why the boy wore the Decepticons toque all summer, but he let it go.

Easier to get distracted by Marley, who was sitting in his lap, crumbling Saltines onto her belly. Eventually, Jake re-emerged, leaf-sprinkled, clutching Theo's old skateboard. Theo looked at the peeling Nirvana stickers and dirty orange wheels and wondered whether he had really ever said the kid could play with it. He suspected that Jake had simply taken it from the basement without asking, but after a moment, he let that slide too.

Jake sat down on the board, then lay down on his back and propelled himself along with his feet. Hanging around with his kids made Theo feel delightfully grown-up. Maybe it was sad that he was only smug in his maturity over a six-year-old scooting backwards across the cement, and a cracker-and-saliva-smeared blind infant. Maybe real grown-ups didn't even use the word *grown-up*.

Marley held a largely intact cracker in both hands, waving it, occasionally sucking on it. She squirmed to put her feet on the step she couldn't see, and couldn't yet stand on unsupported. But she was desperate to walk, constantly pulling herself up on anything she could grasp. Theo had been surprised that she wanted to go places, since how could she know there was anywhere else to go? But Marley had intuited, somehow, the rest of the world, and had started inch-worming towards it, just like on the development charts.

Theo wondered who would turn up first. Rae's workday could spill well past five, or so she said. On the other hand, Colleen, for all her other insanities, was punctual. Or close enough. At 6:19, it was indeed Colleen striding from the bus stop at the corner, which was also at the corner of their overgrown, oversized yard. Her pelt of ginger hair bounced against her back as she walked.

Jake skate-scooted past the bottom of the stairs, close enough for Theo to reach out his socked foot to tap the boy's horizontal stomach. "Look who it is, Jakey."

Marley squawked. Theo wondered if it was the word *look*.

Jake sat up and squawked too. "Dolly. *Dolly!*" And then he was running down the drive to the sidewalk.

Colleen made no eye contact as she stomped along in her short grey school tunic, but when Jake reached her and hugged her waist, she crouched, and said a few words that made him jump and clutch at her flannel shoulders. She tolerated this, but as soon as he let go she straightened. Jake adored Colleen, though no one had ever seen her encourage him, or even answer to the nickname he had given her. She stomped on up the walk, Jake trotting in her tall slender shadow, past the wizened herb garden and bald-headed poppies. She stopped about six feet from Theo and the baby.

"You shouldn't let him run near the road."

Jake plopped down on the board. "I know not to run on. I *know.*"

"He does, actually. We taught him from *The Book of Horrible Accidents.*"

Jake glared. "No. That's not a real book. Mrs. Silver at school just taught us the rules of the road, is all." He picked up an ant and placed it on his palm, watched it crawl.

Colleen's eyes were a flat silver-green, and her gaze rested on Theo as if he were a tree stump or a fire hydrant. "My dad said he'd promised I'd sit for you." She whirled and sat one step lower than Theo, her biceps brushing his knee.

"He was only supposed to ask if you were free – I just mentioned it to him at tennis. You could've said no if you had plans."

She didn't answer and without her looking at him, Theo couldn't gauge if she was listening. "But thanks. It's only dinner, a couple hours. Rae wanted to go. For dinner."

"So go."

The baby squirmed towards Colleen's voice, flailing her now-limp cracker. Theo flipped the baby against his chest. "Rae's not here yet."

"Did she say when she'll be?"

"Just working late, I think." He could feel wet over his left nipple, but Marley's face was pressed too tight to see if it was drool or sick. "She might've called, I guess. The machine's getting a little shaky. But I don't think it's been eating messages yet."

They watched the traffic easing off rush hour. A motorcycle drowned out something Colleen said. At least, he thought he'd heard her voice. He leaned forward, Marley against him. "Sorry, what?"

She turned, gave him the glint of her eyes. "What?"

Joe had mentioned that Colleen had been consistently furious lately. Theo couldn't think of a safe thing to say. "I didn't . . . hear you."

She seemed to consider this. Finally: "It's good you two are going on a date."

Jake, somewhere unseen, was singing. Theo hadn't realized that Colleen knew about the separation. "Well . . . We're going for Vietnamese, this restaurant we love."

"Good for you."

Jake scootched back into view, his voice a high soprano bleat: "Faa-laa-laa-laa-laa, la-la-la-la!"

"Jake, it's summer," Colleen snapped.

"I'm playing pretend."

Marley turned towards the sound of her brother's voice. Often both children seemed unaware that each was not an only child, but occasionally they noticed one other.

"Hey, Marley, hey hey!" Jake danced on the spot, with jazz hands, badly, all the fingers scrunching closed at the same time. The baby waved her own hands, mirror-like enough to be spooky.

"Hey, Dad? I bet Marley would like to ride on your skateboard, eh? I've got a rope an' she could hold onto the rope an' I could pull her around an' – "

"Babies aren't too good at holding on, Jakey. And where did you get a rope?"

"But it's – it's not fair. She never gets to skateboard and I always do. Marley should get a turn."

Colleen muttered, "I dunno about this generosity. The last time I babysat, he grabbed a cinnamon heart out of her mouth."

Marley beamed at the porch rail.

Jake stamped his foot. "When's Mommy getting here?"

Colleen sighed. "We don't know. Phone systems are down."

"No, no, the phone's probably fine, she's just late. Jake, you take Marley for a ride in her stroller, ok? Promise you won't undo the straps?"

"That's not as fun."

"Promise?" Theo knelt awkwardly in front of the stroller and shoved the baby in. It was while he was fumbling with the harness that Theo suddenly realized, "The baby's not supposed to have hard candy! She could choke."

No one answered. The baby kicked him in the face. Not hard, but it took him a moment to recover. "Guys?" He could feel a welt rising hot on his cheekbone. "Where would Marley get a cinnamon heart?"

"We got a whole bucket at the drugstore for two bucks." Jake was already jiggling the stroller, making it nearly impossible to fasten the clasps. The boy had to reach above his own head to reach the handles. This was starting to seem like a bad idea.

"But who gave it to *her*?"

Colleen answered, "Dunno. She'd had it for a while, though – the red was all worn off. Jakey grabbed anyway and put it right in his mouth, dintya, Jakey?"

"Dunno. Can we *go* now, Daddy?"

The clasp slid into place. "No, you cannot push your sister down the stairs." Theo picked up the stroller with both hands, above Jake's head, making Marley *screeeee* with wonder. Once the wheels were on driveway, Jake was zooming off.

"Be careful," Theo wailed.

The weedy lawn slowed them down enough that Theo's heart calmed somewhat. Jake only went a little farther before losing interest in locomotion entirely and flopping down on the grass beside the stroller, apparently talking to Marley.

As Theo sat back down beside Colleen, his bare knee brushed hers. Her skin was cooler than his and he jerked away. "I don't think she'll be long. But I'll pay you for whatever hours you're here, obviously. And the bus fare."

"Good. Are you *sure* she's coming?"

"*Yes.* You know not to give a baby hard candy, right? Despite the expression?"

"*Yes.* Was the date really her idea?"

"*Yes.* But is it still a date if it's with your own wife?"

"Is she still your wife if you're separated?"

This "*Yes!*" was rather sharp but she didn't react. The children were no longer visible, but the hedge was shaking. "She's still my wife."

"But the separation is what makes it a date, anyway. You don't date your wife. You date someone who isn't a sure thing."

"I heard you threw a shoe at your father."

"Not hard. It didn't even bruise. Much."

Theo touched the baby-kick bruise on his own cheek; Joe hadn't mentioned that the shoe had struck flesh. There had been just a tiny rough edge to Joe's voice, the pub was too dim to see a not-much bruise, and Theo was immersed in his own troubles. He asked his babysitter what he'd forgotten to ask his friend: "Why?"

Colleen shrugged. "He was being a dick."

"That takes in a lot of territory. Specific dickness?" He was pleased with that.

"He was on me because I stayed out all night. I was only at Andy's – where does he think I was? And what business is it of his, anyways?"

"Indeed. Indeed." He couldn't think why she was offering this now when the week before she'd refused to tell what was playing on her iPod. Was it a cry for help, a confidence, a compliment to his powers of empathy? Or a challenge? He fished for something to say that wouldn't get a shoe thrown. He tried what he in fact felt, blunt curiosity, hoping it was somehow also the responsible, grown-up thing. He could always report what she said to Joe. "So what did you do?"

"*Do?*"

"Well, you know, all night . . ." He tried to sound knowing but not too knowing – as if teenage sex amused him slightly. But as soon as he said it, Theo was terrified of what she might reveal, what news he might have to break to her father over beers, Joe's quivering mouth only half-obscured by the top of his glass.

"You want to know if I'm still a virgin?"

Now he didn't want to know at all. But he'd started it. "You don't want to discuss it with me?"

"Why would I?"

"Then why tell me where you were? It's not my business if it's not your father's."

"You're not my father." She tipped back on her elbows, looking up at him.

Theo pushed his mouth into a grin. "Nope. Pretty sure not. So, you'll tell me?"

"I didn't say that."

"But will you? It's easy – I'll ask, you answer."

"That's *too* easy."

"Ok. What would be harder? Do you want to embed your sexual status in a crossword clue and have me work it out?"

Her smirk went blank. "No."

Was the joke too complex? Theo was trying to think of a suave explanation when he heard a shriek. He stood abruptly, knees crackling, as the stroller emerged from the bush, leaves in the spokes and through the front bar. The children were both screaming, but with faces neutral, as if the noise were only an assigned task. Jake, now hatless, shoved the thing through the yard, onto the driveway, then out of sight towards the backyard. Theo took a step after them.

Colleen said, "He does that all the time when I sit. He's a good stroller-pusher."

Theo sat back down on his step. He really hadn't wanted to pursue or punish.

Colleen said, "It's six twenty-nine."

"She'll come. She's coming."

"Wouldn't she have called if she was running late? She's a half-hour late."

"She didn't . . ." Colleen didn't interrupt, so Theo was forced to finish the sentence. ". . . didn't say *six* exactly. She said *after work.*"

She rolled her eyes, but not in a teenaged who-cares way. This was an adult, pitying eye-roll, such as any of his tougher friends would have given such banal manipulation. Joe was not one of his tougher friends.

"So, really, she could show up anytime. And I rushed for nothing."

"She usually gets home *around* six, anyway."

"How do you know her *usually* if you haven't lived with her for six months?"

"She still has the same job. And we've talked since then. We talk all the time."

Colleen silently tugged her tunic over her knees, over and over. It wasn't long enough not to flick right back up over bare round knees. Flick up, tug down, flick up –

"Stop that."

"It doesn't fit," Colleen said without stopping. "I'm going to get in trouble on uniform day for showing my panties on the stairs. They'll think I'm like those hiked-up whores who do it on purpose."

"It's just because you're tall, though . . . right?"

"Right. But the VP is an asshole."

"I am the king," Jake announced. The kids had re-appeared in front of the garage without Theo noticing. Jake was standing on the underseat rack of the stroller, his head between the handlebars. "I am the master of everybody."

"Jake, you can be king with your feet on the ground, please. And where's your toque? We can't buy another if it's lost – they're not for sale in summer."

Marley's tiny fat hands waved like a conductor's.

"Marley is my slave. I am in charge. I am the king."

"Jake, really. Down, now."

Jake stood perfectly still and screamed, "You aren't the king. Where's Mommy?" He began to bounce on the rack, bending and straightening his knees, not actually jumping, though the whole contraption jiggled. Marley tossed her head as if to see what disaster had befallen her. Her navy eyes were humungous.

"Mommy's on her way from work *right now* and she'll be *so mad* to see you jumping on your sister's stroller."

A bark of laughter from Colleen.

Marley began to punch the air, loudly cooing, "Ohmmy ohmmy ohmmy!"

Startled by the noise, Jake jerked backwards, fell, heaved up and grabbed the stroller to push it full-tilt back into the bushes.

Colleen nodded slowly, as though her chin were weighted. "They say divorce is always hardest on the children."

Theo jolted to his feet, conscious even as he did of how awkwardly similar his motion was to the six-year-old's a moment ago. "We're not getting divorced, we're *working through this*. What did Joe tell you, anyway?" Theo wasn't actually sure he was right about the divorce, and less sure he could convince Colleen, who was quite capable of eavesdropping on his sad drunk conversations with Joe. Or just reading his mind.

A breeze lifted snarls of ginger curls around her shoulders. "He said it's a trial separation. And that I shouldn't ask about it."

"And how are you doing on that?"

"Yeah, Joe accidentally put the hydro bill into a recycling bin instead of a mailbox yesterday. I don't obey him on principle. Am I getting dinner tonight?"

Theo willed his ribcage to expand with air, then contract to press out all the frustration and tension and rage. He'd been doing Rae's yoga DVDs after the kids were asleep, but by then he was so exhausted he might not quite have had it right.

"There's, yeah, some scalloped turnips in the fridge, just microwave 'em. And tofu steaks from the weekend, if you want. The kids will probably just want the turnips, but give them the tofu if they ask."

Colleen put her face on her knees. "The kids will *want scalloped turnips?*"

"It's a free meal, Colleen."

She raised her head, suddenly bright and interested. "Are we going to argue?"

"What?"

"You sounded . . . exasperated. If I'm mean, will you be mean back?"

"I wasn't being mean, I just didn't want you to – "

"Yeah yeah yeah. Better than Joe, just sitting there like a lump of – "

"That's why you threw the shoe? Because your father is an insufficient debater?"

"He didn't even make a sound when it hit him. That's how I know it didn't hurt."

"That's not a way to know. Especially with Joe."

"She's not *coming*, you know. This is a joke."

He sighed, and then tried to make the sigh into a yoga breath. "You can't make me angry, and you can't make me think Rae won't come. People get held up at work. Buses get stuck. Those are reasonable explanations. And there are others."

"Not for why she wouldn't have called and used two 3-cent cellphone minutes to tell you that."

"There might be something wrong with the – "

"There *isn't*. Just for argument's sake say there isn't."

"Fine. But how do you explain why she'd *ask me* to dinner and then not come?"

"Cruelty?"

"Separation doesn't mean Rae hates me. Even divorce wouldn't mean that."

"Doesn't have to have hate involved. Might not even be about you, or anyone. Some people are just naturally cruel."

"Rae is not cruel," he said fast and involuntarily, words expelled like the *whoosh* of breath that would have come out had Colleen punched him in the stomach.

"No?"

"Marley, sit *down*. It won't *work* if you *do* that."

The children were at the backyard gate, almost behind the porch. Marley was flopped forward over her chair-bar, with Jake in front of her, a long stick in his right hand, drawn up as if to stab. But of course he would not do that. Theo gathered himself to speak sharply, to take the stick away, to parent.

Without turning her eyes from Marley and Jake, Colleen murmured, "Do you think *I'm* cruel?"

Theo froze half-standing, in a kind of pre-modern hunch. "Cruel?"

"Because I threw a shoe at my father, who is basically a nice person that just doesn't know what the hell is going on? Should I just have let him be, in his ignorance?"

Theo felt his shoulders relax, let himself sink back onto the step. He suddenly knew what to say. "I do think you should have let him be. Because the punishment didn't educate him, did it? There should only be punishment when it has the capacity to reform. Otherwise it's just energy wasted, pain – cruelty. Joe learned nothing about your wish for privacy from that shoe, so nothing was gained. You were cruel."

Colleen seemed to slip backwards without actually moving, shrink into herself. But then she said, "So you'll learn nothing, then, if Rae stands you up tonight?"

"Colleen, I told you, she'll – "

"There is no lesson she could teach you, that she could be hoping to teach you, by not showing up tonight?"

He gave her his gaze again, though he was starting to suspect he shouldn't. "What could I learn, from that?"

She wiggled her whole body, a wave from ankles to ears. "Oh, you know, that she doesn't love you, that you shouldn't be married to her."

He ignored the soap-operatic tone, the high-schooler's conception of marriage as a poker-hand that can be won or lost once and never replayed. He concentrated on *she doesn't love you,* tried to hear it as a statement, and then to believe it.

It didn't take – he just pictured his wife bent over a tortoise skeleton at the ROM, then her pacing the living room with

Marley in her arms and graham cracker crumbs down both their sweaters. Then Rae with her head thrown back at orgasm, mouth open pink, dark hair strewn on an orange-juice stained pillow.

"Maybe I got the date wrong. Or she did." He was pleased to hear ease in his voice, dreamy absent-mindedness, and assurance.

"I'm not a virgin."

He choked on air.

She gazed at him, the green of her eyes greyer than her father's, more muted, although not dull. Like a camouflaged python. "It's your turn to talk."

"That's not a rule that's strictly observed."

"I'm observing it."

"So . . . are you ok with that?"

"Well, I wasn't *raped* or anything."

"I'm just not certain what you want me to do with this information, Colleen."

"*Do*? Does anyone *do* anything with information? It's just for knowing."

"Some information, yes, requires a reaction."

"So what could be the reaction I want? What could I want you to do?"

"I can't tell you what you want."

"I'm not asking that. I didn't know I could want *anything*. I'm asking you to give me a list of options and I'll choose."

"Well . . ." He knew he was being baited, but Jake was at the hedge unfastening Marley from her stroller, his best meal all week had been turnips, and his wife was a) in her Post-it feathered cubical, b) in her snug bachelor apartment, eating spaghetti out of a tin and thinking of the lesson she had taught him, c) fucking a stranger or, at least, a stranger to Theo, or d) something he couldn't ever imagine.

The worst part was that he knew d) was correct and no matter what course the future took, he would never know what Raeanne had been doing at six that evening. At least Colleen was there, with her ugly dress high on her straight narrow thigh, which was parallel his Zellers jeans. He loved her because she was there, speaking to him, passing the time. This had always been his undoing.

"Well, Colleen, if you don't see any options, there probably aren't any. Really."

"That's how it works?"

"In this case. It's not like a menu, the lemonade or the boiler-maker. These are internal choices, about what you want."

"Boilermaker?"

"It's a drink, a beer and a shot . . . It doesn't matter, you're too young to drink."

"I am?"

"Oh, god, what part of teenager class did you miss? You don't tell your dad's friends this stuff."

She nodded as though taking notes on the customs of foreign tribes.

". . . .unless you are seeking some sort of reaction from them, which you claim you can't even imagine."

"But *you* choose your reaction. So how should I know what you'll do?"

"So you told me about losing your virginity . . . to see what I'd do?"

For the first time that afternoon answers didn't bounce out of her throat the moment he stopped speaking. She flicked the skirt up, down, up. Finally, with the whisper of a smile on her chap-stick lips, she said, "More or less."

Theo let the silence slide on. The children had laid themselves down on the grass, side by side, either sleeping or pretending to sleep, probably not dead. He didn't know how Jake had wrestled Marley out of the stroller, got her lying supine in the grass, high blades nearly covering her pink arms and legs. Jake himself was facedown in the green, apparently taking no questions.

35

It was nearly seven o'clock by the thin silver hands of his watch.

"Dolly . . ."

Colleen smiled more broadly in answer, a half nod.

Theo turned his head to the west, where his wife would come from, and to the pink hot beams of the setting sun. He wondered what she would see if she came walking down the street right now. Or whenever she finally did.

To: All onsite employees; all temporary employees;
all telecommute staff
CC: Belinda Martin
From: Human Resources Administration
Re: Personnel change

                                    Tuesday 3:06 p.m.

This is to inform all staff that Mai-Nam Stephens has left
the Technical Support team to pursue other endeavours;
we wish her all the best. Please be assured that all calls
to the support team or emails to support@dream.com will
continue to receive a quick and helpful response.

Please feel free to contact anyone in Human Resources if
you have any questions or concerns.

COMPLIMENTARY
YOGA

THE BIRTHDAY COFFEE BREAK for Suyin is awful – Grig jams the coffee maker, forgets the English words to "Happy Birthday," and no one eats anything. All the customer service reps show up because she's supervisor, but they leave almost right away. Suyin just says, "Ah, thank you so much, guys" and goes back to her office. Grig was so happy to pull Suyin in the birthday-duties draw – he needs to make up for his shitty performance evaluation, plus she's got such a hot little ass – and now it's just a wasted forty dollars on Cinnabon. He ends up giving them all to Wayne, the big black guy who sits in the call-station beside his.

"Why people don't like Cinnabons, Wayne?"

"*Every*one likes Cinnabons. But most CSRs are single chicks, dude, and they're not gonna risk getting fat with this shit." Wayne carefully sharpies WAYNE on each box.

"I hate fat chicks." Grig thinks for a moment. "Suyin has no boyfriend?"

Wayne shoves the boxes into the crowded staff fridge and tries to smash it shut. A magnet shaped like a sushi roll falls on the floor. "Someone fuck a tightass like that? Not likely." The fridge finally seals, but they hear something thump, then crash, within.

*

At home, Grig bothers Mariska like her younger brother, which people sometimes mistake him for. Usually people think they're at least from the same country. But they aren't, and they speak only English at home because Mariska says a good Ukrainian doesn't speak Russian even though she totally can. If he even starts a conversation with *zdrastvuite,* she talks all day about what a putz Yushchenko is.

"Do you worry about being fatso?" he asks her from the open bathroom doorway.

"No!" She is wringing water out of her pink sweater, her long pink nails delicately splayed. "You tell me I should?"

"No!" Grig looks at her ass, feels her glare, looks away. "Canadian girls worry."

Mariska hangs her sweater on the clothesline between their faces. "Canadian girls are fat – they should worry."

"Some girls are not fat and still they worry to keep the fat away . . . ." Grig knows he said something a Canadian would laugh at, but Mariska's English is even worse than his.

Mariska squeezes a pink lace thong until the whole thing disappears in her palm, then flips it over the line. "Grig, you think I am fatso!!"

"No! I think you are skinny girl. How do you do that, is what I want to know?"

Mariska's nearly invisible eyebrows twist and scrunch.

"What you eat? To be so . . ." He makes the hourglass gesture. She has a bra in her hand now, tightly squeezing. Grig puts his hands down. ". . . beautiful."

"I eat normal food, but not like cow. You see me, I don't hide nowhere – breakfast is the yoghurt and the Corn Pops. Lunch – " she pronounces it *lunk;* Grig wonders if he does this, too " – at work is sometime chicken, sometime shrimp. At home, maybe potato in coat – in jacket? I like potatoes anyhow . . . ."

Grig realizes that this is one of the things Mariska could talk about for hours, and he's not actually learning what he wanted to know.

"So you eat normal food like everybodies . . . ."

"Like you, Grig. I eat what you eat, don't I? We have same fridge, same stove."

"I – " Grig throws his hands down across his small soft body. "I do not look like you. So what you do – exercises?"

Mariska laughs, rough and breathy, with her mouth wide and tongue peeking, reminding him that he once found her hot. That feeling is gone now. He knows her too well, knows the ease with which he could have her, since she's had everyone. That makes her unfuckable.

"Grig, we not all have the perfect English for the cushion desk jobs! Some of us have to run fast with heavy trays so the managers don't yell and the customers don't pinch asses. Jack Astor's is exercise gym, all right."

"Oh." Grig nods. Marishka knows nothing that applies to Suyin, it seems.

"But the womens who come to the restaurant . . ." she walks into the hall, not looking back to see if he follows ". . . they worry about skinny. They don't eat bread, don't eat croutons, talk talk talk about the yoga. They put their mats under the table to trip me."

"Mats?" he asks, trailing her to the front door.

Mariska rolls her eyes; she was like a sister he couldn't yell at or shove. "Skinny rich bitches are lazy, but still they must exercise, so they do exercises lying down. Is like exercise nap, to get stretchy. For princesses, for rich girls."

"Stretchy?"

"Yah. If you using my computer to Google, take your shoes off in my room."

*

What he wants happens in the worst way possible. Suyin sends him an email – no mass-mail, addressed only to him – but it's "feedback." His call logs are bad. He's had lot of hang-ups, lot of escalations, lots of confusion. "I be right back in the queue-up" is listed as off-script dialogue that the subscribers to *Dream Parent* couldn't comprehend.

He has to go see her. Just the two of them in her tiny office that is glass on two sides, so all the CSRs know Grig and Suyin are alone together. Suyin sits facing the glass corner and motions for Grig to sit on the opposite side of a table so narrow they could kiss across it without standing up. But the table is scattered with goldenrod complaint forms, Suyin's face is red, and it's clear there will be no kiss. Maybe not clear through the window though – maybe everyone thinks they've got something hot going on.

"I think you know . . . probably know . . . why I . . . Don't you?" She sounds nervous – that he is so close?

The thing to do is be cool. "I have a few problems, I know, Suyin." He has practiced pronouncing her name, gets it perfect: soo-YIN. "I must do better."

"Yes, exactly." She brightens and finally looks at him. "We need to go over some things."

He says nothing, because she has spoken too fast and he was looking at her chest. She is wearing a soft minty sweater with a tiny V-neck – too small to even show a hint of a breast. Wayne is a little right, she is tight-assed, a bit frigid in her clothes.

When he returns his gaze to her face, Grig realizes she has said more things and he doesn't know what they are. He says, "I do better."

"Yeees. You *must* be more patient with customers. When you interrupt, you not only miss info, it costs you the customer's trust. People don't like being cut off."

"I must get the call-times down, yes? And many who call, they are old lonelies, talking and talking, pointless."

Suyin's back stiffens, and her breasts point higher. "Not pointless. Many times, I think you'll find if you take a bit more time to find out exactly what the issue is – "

"I am a good listener, is not a problem. I am caring to hear. I am a good guy."

Suyin breathes out sharply, as if some dust had gone up her nose. "I know that, Grigori. But you need to concentrate on being *useful* to customers. Your goodness is no good if they can't get what they want."

Suyin has sped up talking again, but he catches that she has called him *Grigori*, which no one says in English. So prissy. Aren't they friends? He threw her a party.

After a while, she picks up a new page and says, "Ok? Ring!"

He should have listened. He could have understood, if he really focused. The problem is that focusing takes a lot of energy, and he can shut it off too easily. In Cherkessk, he woke a hundred times a year to hear his parents yelling at each other, or drunken talk and songs in the street. In Russian, he couldn't not listen. The eyes close but the ears don't – words always got in and he always understood them, angry, pointless, incoherent, anything, pouring into his ears and brain unstoppably. English requires effort, which means when he relaxes, leans back, lets a stray thought lead his mind, he often drifts so far from the conversation. there might be no way back.

"Ring?"

"Yes!" Grig is so fucked.

"Ok . . ." She points her small finger at her ear like a gun, and says, "Ring-ring!" and he gets that she's pretending to be a phone – it's a practice phone call. He hates these bullshit games, and yet Suyin's breasts are perfect, even in the dumb sweater.

He beams at her, points his own small finger at his ear, and says, "Ring!"

Suyin does not smile back. She whispers, as if they had an audience she is protecting him from, "No, *you* answer."

He chuckles, then thinks, then flushes. "Hello?"

Still she is silent, as if the invisible audience prevents her explaining what is wrong. "Hello?" she says to her finger. "Who is this?"

"Oh! I never make that mistake on live line. No, never." He shakes his head.

Suyin just nods and this time he understands that she will not stop this pretend phone call for anything. He feels suddenly that she is just processing him like a month-end report, not treating him as her office-friend Grig. He wonders if there are cameras in the ceiling or some other reason beyond her being a silly bitch.

"Thanks for calling Dream Magazines today. How may I help you dream?"

"I am so angry! The mail carrier informed me that yet *again* my copy of *Dream Retirement* is not in his sack! This is outrageous! That was the November issue . . . ."

Her voice has gone shrill as a cat, though her face is blank and her eyes focused on her page. Her soft sweetness is all gone – she is completely unfuckable now.

"Well? Are you going to *do* anything about it? *Well?*"

He will answer her, polite, professional, *Canadian*, in a moment. For that moment, he just sits there, hating her.

*

A lot of the guys he went to grade 12 with – he was only in Canada for grade 12, his father had thought that was enough – are still around Scarborough and they sometimes hang out. But this weekend no one calls with any invitations for clubs, any cheap weed or pills, any video-game nights in someone's basement apartment.

So he is awake and sober on a Sunday morning for the first time in ages. Mariska has figured out how to password-protect her wireless, so he can't look at porn on the internet. Which is fine, actually – he jerks off imagining Suyin's pretty little breasts, her pretty mouth all tight and prissy, imagining holding her head back and shoving inside, pumping into her throat. It is wonderful when he shoots off, and then terrible when he's just lying there in his old Vanier T-shirt with a slimy sock in his hand.

He gets up and thinks about showering but just gets dressed. He puts the sock in Mariska's laundry. She won't notice until after she's washed it, and by then she won't be able to tell what was on it.

His friend Tomas works at a jerk chicken place downtown. Grig can get free plantains and shoot the shit for a while, guaranteed, which gives the day a point, a bit.

Tomas is a big Brazilian guy with a tattoo of a spiderweb creeping out the collar of his shirt. They had autoshop together in school. "Grig, *que pasa*?" he yells when the door jingles. Grig just waves – he's tired of faking any language shit.

The gospel reggae is too crackling loud and the floor is sticky and all the customers are stupid. A little white paper bag of plantains slides across the table. "What's shakin'?" Tomas flops into a plastic chair, making it rock back and almost dump him.

"Not much." Grig shoves a plaintain chunk in his mouth. When he bites, steam escapes and scalds his tongue. It hurts so bad he has to spit it out but there's no napkin or anything so he winds up with this hot slimy gob in the palm of his hand. He shouldn't have gone for it so fast. He should have had breakfast. The music swoops high.

"Jesus, man." Tomas goes and gets him a napkin from the counter. With his long legs, the restaurant is barely one stride. He plonks back down and Grig wraps the dead food, smiling weakly.

His tongue feels raw, tastes like blood.

"Job all right? Ladies?"

"It's the same, right? Lad*ee* and job, same."

"Yeah?" Tomas's heavy black eyebrow is like a cat arching its back.

"Serious. Because my lady is my boss, see? It's convenient."

Tomas belly-laughs and, because *now* is the exact right moment, fishes the exact right piece of plantain out of the bag and pops it into his mouth. Grig sighs – Tomas never does anything stupid, gets any pussy he wants. It's annoying. At least Tomas buys the story about Suyin – it's more fun to talk about her as if she's in the bag than to tell the truth. Although Tomas might have had some advice.

"She hawt?" Tomas crunches his food around his words. "Tell me ass, tell me tits, tell me . . . belly ring? I love those damn belly rings."

"Not much ass, tits very nice, belly ring . . ." the details of even a simple lie always trip him up – would she? Her hair is so tidy, her nails so clean ". . . no piercings at all."

"Woah, a goodie girl."

Grig grins and dares to eat a plantain. "Yeah, but not totally tight, no. Not at all."

They grin together, then chew. The plantain is the perfect temperature now, flaking hot and sweet on his tongue.

"She does yoga." Mariska is always right about these things; it doesn't feel even like a lie. "She's streeeeettttttchy." He throws his arms back, thrusts out his chest till it's as broad as Tomas's, wriggles his eyebrows.

Tomas smacks his hand on the table. "All *right*, brother."

Vicki strides into the restaurant, to their table, and climbs onto Tomas's lap. She's not his girlfriend – Tomas bangs everyone – but she's around a lot. She's singing along with the music, "Don't let nobody come between you and your god . . . ." She sounds good.

"Grig's got hisself a wo*man*!" Tomas yells, sliding his palm under Vicki's baggy-denim thigh. "A yoga woman. Now that's hot. Why don't you do some yoga, Vicki?" He slaps her ass gently.

Vicki gives Grig a big-teeth smile. "Yoga is very healthy, very natural, very love-lee. You should get her to take me."

Grig feels his eyelashes snap back, and imagines the two women together in a gym shower, Vicki all long lime-green nails and round brown ass and squealing laughter, while tiny Suyin dances around her, her usually smooth hair soaked and tangled.

"I – she lives out by the airport, near work, so she's . . ."

"*Gawd,* the *sub*urbs. But you are, too! You can be happy together in the *sub*urbs."

Tomas laughs, his stomach bouncing Vicki up and down. "Scarborough and Mississauga are different sides of the city, Vic, and different besides. Right, Griggy?"

He nods. Since the arrival of Vicki, Tomas has abandoned the plantains and Grig is ploughing through them, chewing rapidly now that they are cool.

"You must get this suburban girl a *pres*ent!" Vicki slaps the table.

"I gotta go back to work. Break's over." Tomas starts to stand and Vicki leans her weight on her forearms on the table, standing on tiptoe, ass in the air, as he slips away.

She looks into Grig's eyes. Vicki has dark hair with thick-painted gold highlights, big dark eyes, and an unplaceable accent. In school, everyone wanted her. "I will help you find a present."

Grig glances over Vicki's shoulder at her ass. "You don't must."

"I *want* to shop and I got nothing to shop for. Let's go." It's a whole subway stop to walk, and Vicki keeps singing about the work God wants them to do the whole way.

*

The mall is well enough lit but it always feels dark. Three guys bump into them. They all wear soft dark hoodies, loose jeans, big white shoes – they look just like Grig and Vicki, and when they pull back apologizing, all three seem to see the resemblance. One boy's "Sorry" stops at "suh" and sounds a lot like "suck," but they nod respectfully at the rhinestone V lodged between Vicki's breasts (even in winter, she keeps her North Face jacket zipped only half), wander off, eyes downward.

Vicki crosses her arms and adjusts herself. They walk on, and Vicki keeps getting sexy looks. Grig gets envious ones. What is it with all these beautiful useless women that he is always surrounded by but can never fuck?

"Lululemon is the best for yoga things, someone told me that. It is all very sexy, but quality. Is she seriously into yoga?"

"Well she is . . . a serious girl," Grig says carefully. He pictures Suyin's eyes, big and dark as she slid his performance warning towards him on the table.

The lights seem a bit brighter in Lululemon, but it could be just because the walls are green, blue, red. On the racks are shirts shaped like breasts, same as at any girl store. Peppy tiny girls flit between them. Vicki blends in, though she is bigger than the other girls and her shoulder bag bonks one of them in the face.

Another girl dances over to Vicki. "If you have any questions at all, just ask . . . ."

"Oh, *I* don't do yoga." Vicki glances back at her ass as if she were smiling at a friend. "*He's* shopping for his girlfriend."

If Suyin were his girlfriend, he would have to drop his elbow almost to his ribcage to put an arm around her. If Suyin were his girlfriend, she would help him at work without being mean, without him needing to ask or even knowing he was being helped – like magic, just by being there, talking to him, all the time in her perfect English.

"She does a lot of . . . yoga." He's picturing Suyin doing the twisty sexy things in the pictures on the wall. This lie has been going on all day. Soon, he knows, he will forget the conversation with Mariska entirely.

The salesgirl asks him, "Here?"

"What?" He glances around – bins of pants, halters on mannequins, little women. He doesn't see anything that helps him. "What?"

"Does she know about our complimentary yoga on Sunday mornings? It's a really great treat for the mindbodysoul?" Her unpainted nail points to the calendar on the wall. Every Sunday does read "Complimentary Yoga!!!"

When the woman drifts away, he asks Vicki what *complimentary* means.

"Free!" she whispers, as if the staff and other shoppers were listening.

"Oh, good." He is fingering a pink halter top, imagining somehow mentioning complimentary yoga to Suyin and her somehow not knowing where the Eaton's Centre is, and him somehow going out to Mississauga to get her and take her here. He could hang out with Tomas while the class was on. No fucking way was he doing yoga.

He glances down at the pink fabric and sees the price label – $52.00CAD.

For a minute he forgets the whole lie, the fact that Suyin is probably not a yoga-doer, and certainly not his girlfriend. Suyin is suddenly a bratty big-shot, demanding presents he cannot afford. He almost says, *That bitch!* Actually he sorta does whisper it, but no one hears.

He puts down the shirt and walks further into the shop. $90 for black stretchy sweatpants like at Zellers. Even the T-shirts are more than twice what he's got in his wallet. Finally he finds a bin of small things, and small is cheaper. When Vicki gooses him from behind, he is looking for the price tag on a pink lace thong.

"Oh-ho, she's *that* kind. *I* see. Got yourself a yoga whore, eh, Grig?"

Then he's buying it – at the green-and-wood-paneled cashier's desk buying a lacy strand to go up the tiny ass of a girl he's never spoken to except about call times and scripts, all because he's a liar living in a porno fantasy. At least the panties only cost $14.

*

Owning them – the panties – makes things way weirder. He's got them jammed in the bottom drawer of the filing cabinet he uses as a bureau, but all night in his room he thinks about them. Maybe he will take them out to look at, hold, rub against, but he doesn't. Maybe he'll return them, because even fourteen bucks plus tax would help with rent. He knows someone would be able to tell if he touches them too much.

It's also so weird looking at Suyin at work now, like seeing a girl from a porno site just walking down the street (this has never happened to Grig, but he has imagined it many times). He thinks her hips are probably narrower than the small-size he chose.

Mainly she doesn't even look at him. They only talk about his call times, logsheets, scripts. She aims her words at the wall behind his head. How serious does she think he takes this stupid job, that telling him he keystroked a credit-card number wrong is worth all her silly drama, her slanting eyes looked down, her cheeks blooming rose, saying it's going to be a dock in pay if it happens again – because it costs the company, because he needs to take her feedback seriously, because because.

He has to think about her in his off-hours, whether he wants to or not, because now too many people think they know about her. He made the mistake of asking Mariska if she thought the panties were cute, and now she won't stop asking why he's home watching *Sex Rehab* every night since he has a girlfriend. Finally he tells her that Suyin lives with her parents, and their relationship is a secret because he isn't – what is she? He momentarily panics, then says, *Chinese*.

Tomas says he's having a house party, which is fucked because Tomas don't even have a house, just a basement flat like Grig, only at least with no Mariska. On Grig's Facebook wall he writes, "Bring your girl!" He can't just write an excuse on Tomas's wall because that puts the lie in public. If someone from work sees Tomas's post and says, "I didn't know you had a girl," he can say

Tomas is wrong, crazy, whatever. But if Grig writes, "Suyin is sick, can't come" or even, "My girl is sick," then he can never take it back. The party is in a week. Grig stays up worrying, watching reruns of *Sex Rehab*.

At work, at the end of his Thursday shift, he gets a call from a lady whose English is worse than his. It ends with her screaming that the postman never comes, the postman is garbage, GARBAGE. She sounds about one hundred and three but she sure can scream and he yells right back at her, "You don't fucking yell at me, bitch. I'm helping you."

Then it's creepy because Suyin's voice breaks in and he knows that the threat to sometimes monitor them is true. Even as Suyin's smooth anywhere accent is calming the crazy lady down, he is realizing he's more fucked than he knew because he sometimes very quietly tells a caller that they don't know what they are talking about, the magazine will come tomorrow, that the order has already been corrected, the problem solved, all things back good. Just to get a moment's peace, to check Facebook on his phone, to go take a shit, just some peace.

Nothing happens that afternoon – he somehow gets through the last half-hour with no calls and just goes without even seeing Suyin. The next morning, he has a new date in his Outlook calendar and realizes that Suyin will fire him when she shows up at their eleven o'clock appointment. He doesn't have anything to do – his station has been shut down or something, no calls are coming in.

He dicks around on his cellphone for a while. He's going to have to cut off the internet capability, he can't afford it. Tomas and Vicki are writing on each other's Facebook walls every day now, practically – if it gets around that they're dating, Tomas will totally lose his player status. Suyin is walking around the CSR room, talking to people, picking up timesheets because it's Friday. She's going to fucking fire him never even knowing how into her he is, how good a boyfriend he would be.

Suyin would forgive him for one silly little slip. It's her boss, he forgets that bitch's name, but she is a total bitch. Suyin is a sweetheart who likes him. She would never hurt him. She's probably really sad and upset that she has to do this – because she doesn't want to hurt him and because she will miss him. She doesn't even know how he feels, or that in his head, heart, bottom drawer, he's already her perfect boyfriend.

She comes up behind him and says, "Grig." His headset, which he hadn't even realized he was holding, hits the floor. She scoops it up, says, "Let's go," then turns without waiting for an answer.

He watches her walk away, picturing her striding ahead of him on the bumpy asphalt pathway in front of Tomas's basement stairs, on the way to the party. Suyin's hips would be swaying the way they totally aren't now, and he would know the sway came from the rub of a lace thong in her ass.

She has disappeared down the hall. He finds her in the CSR conference room, standing at the table, head bent. She looks like a priest, praying on her feet.

"Hello, Suyin."

She makes eye-contact but doesn't smile as she walks towards him. It seems like she's walking straight into his arms, but at the last moment she deeks left and taps the door shut behind him. Then she pulls back to arm's length, still holding eye-contact. It's very sexy or, at least, it could be.

"Hello, Grigori. I think you know why I wanted to speak to you alone."

Her words sound like a porno, but when he takes a step towards her, she goes back to the table and reads from her file folder.

"You've been on probation since our feedback meeting on March 23. I'm sorry to say that since then there was an incident that forces me to terminate your contract."

She is reading aloud. Someone has put her to this, clearly – it is an assignment she hates. She hates the department bosses and

Dream Inc. and everything that forces them to be apart. Her hand grip the paper in front of her chest. "I have to ask you to leave the building now." The page rattles but she keeps it between them. Her eyes seem teary.

"Is ok, Suyin." He is so tense that he makes an old mistake – everyone knows "It is." "Don't worry." He takes a step forward. He wants to reach out and take the paper, tell her don't worry, he's the sort of guy who has gotten her an invitation to a big party and bought her a present. She will be so grateful. On Sunday after the party and all the fucking in the pink lace thong, he will take her to complimentary yoga at the mall, and stand quietly in a corner watching her twist and bend. Then go home and fuck again. On Monday they will come to work holding hands above the parking brake in Suyin's car, and she will explain to the bosses that they are fuckers, and give him his headset back.

"Of course." She lets her hand fall. "I'm sure you'll find another job soon."

His fingertips are almost touching her grey-sweatered arm when he registers what she has said. "No. Is better I stay here. You'll help." He smiles encouragingly.

"No . . . the decision is . . . is firm. That feedback was your final warning. I'm afraid nothing else . . ." How could she let the bosses fuck her, fuck *them* around like this?"

"Do not do this, Suyin. You know I love you."

He is close to her now, can feel her breath against his chest, or thinks he can. She takes a step to the side.

"What did you say?"

Something pounds hard in his belly, down low near his dick but not sexy.

"There's this party I will take you to, my friend Tomas, he's a fun guy, you'll see. And his girlfriend, Vicki. I have told them all about you."

"All about me what? Whatever would you tell them about me?"

He is confused, tired, can't remember if *whatever* is the same as what. He has been so good to her, so sweet and polite, not like with those Scarborough whores. Yet she is trying to get rid of him. He could make her so happy, buy her presents, take her places.

"I asked . . . I wanted them to help buy you a present. I wanted to pick the right thing." This is true, more or less.

"Grig . . . it wouldn't be . . . appropriate for me to accept a gift from you."

He wants to tell her it's appropriate, that he loves her and she cannot betray his beautiful love, but it's a thong and a tight-ass like her would never understand the long day downtown and stupid nosy Vicki and all the complimentary yoga he has in mind. It's hard for him to get his thoughts organized to tell her in English, but he will. He closes his eyes to think but then he hears the *snick* of the doorknob turning and he opens his eyes and slams the door shut with his palm.

"Grig! I have to – "

"I love you, Suyin, you don't fucking – " This is not what he meant to be saying, and she is flushed and water is tricking down her face and she goes for the door again and if she leaves she'll be out of his life and he won't see her pretty, tight-ass little face and he knocks the door shut again.

"Grig, what are you *doing*?"

She's crying, crying!

"I'm sorry, Suyin, don't cry. I love you." He reaches out his arms and she flinches but she's in the corner by the door and she can't pull back. She's afraid, that's what she is, the stupid cunt, afraid of *him*, when he loves her and buys her gifts. He puts his arms around her, presses her wet face into the front of his shirt to dry her tears. He hugs her so tight.

THE ANONYMOUS
PARTY

"MA, I'M HOME." Yaël took off her steel-grey trench, hung it carefully on its hook, then bent to unzip her steel-grey presentation boots.

Her mother was sitting on the hall bench beside her, rubbing her left foot. "I see you. You gonna to eat here tonight?"

"Yeah, but early. I'm going out." She knocked over a boot, bit her lips, righted it, all without looking at her mother. Yaël was anxious. To go to a party with graduate students, to be introduced as Sasha's girlfriend – these were huge wardrobe questions, a totally new hair problem. And her longest black miniskirt was in the wash and the autumn humidity would get into her hair if she didn't straight-iron it, and was all this even worth it for another woman? Her mother sat watching Yaël take off her pearl-button earrings, her presentation watch, her hairclip, until Yaël couldn't stand it anymore and whirled down the hall to turn on the shower.

When she came back her mother was putting her shoes under the bench, and had to ask over her shoulder, "Did the logo presentation go all right?"

Yaël started unbuttoning her blouse. "Yeah, of course. Abey home?"

"Working late again. You know how fall is. I'll fix your dinner. Who you going out with? Lahley and Jane? Who's driving?"

"Sasha. It's a party. We're gonna meet there." Yaël gave up on the buttons and whipped her shirt over her head, muffling *meet* and *there.* Her mother would have watched Yaël's whole life on cable, in real time, had there been such a station. Yaël would have been happy to limit their conversations to food and clothes, but when her mother asked, she always answered, an involuntary reflex. She knew if her mother ever asked her point-blank if she was sexually attracted to females, she would answer yes. But her mother probably wouldn't ask her that.

Chien came up and since she was taking her clothes off anyway, Yaël gave him a pat and let him rub his woolly head against her nylon leg. "I've got to be there by eight. Don't put sauce on anything, ok?" Then she unzipped her tweed skirt, let it slip down, kicked it up into her hand and marched to the bathroom, wondering whether lesbians said *girlfriend* or *partner,* and whether that was the same as what intellectuals said. Probably.

*

Sasha had said come any time after eight, but Yaël had spent the day discussing fonts and pantones and swirls for the logo, smiling hard at people she didn't like. She was tired enough that she'd have to go early to make the preparation worthwhile, if it would be at all.

She thought of the raised-eyebrow thrill of a man's face upon seeing her best – hair, breasts, eyebrows, thighs. She would miss those eyebrows, that twist of a man's desiring mouth before he kissed her. But she was not saying *never again* to men. And despite Sasha's sneakers and books and intellect, her face was probably still capable of opening into wonder for a perfect toss of perfect hair. Yaël thought it could happen.

*

Yaël came downstairs in her blue silky robe and blue Chinese slippers, her blonde hair dripping polka dots on her shoulders. Her mother was waiting in the kitchen, surrounded by food. Yaël ignored the boiled potatoes in the sink and opened the oven to stab one of the turkey cutlets with a fork. The oven door crashed shut and her mother sucked in a breath but didn't say anything. Yaël dumped broccoli onto her plate, then put a tiny spoonful of sauce over the meat. "It's not spicy, is it? The sauce?" Yaël looked hard. She couldn't see anything in the goop except flecks of freeze-dried onion, but some spices could dissolve.

"It's not spicy." Her mother had changed into a housedress with snaps up the front and slippers that were like Yaël's but green. She opened a drawer and took her time rummaging for the potato peeler, clattering around. The housedress was not flattering but Yaël had never come up with a way to tell her mother that.

Yaël sat down and cut a piece of meat with only a little sauce on it. She had her mouth full when her mother said, "So who's this Sasha?"

She swallowed. The sauce was a little spicy, a little sharp, too. Maybe paprika. It wasn't worth starting an argument over. Neither was her mother's question. Yaël dug her fork into a broccoli. "Sasha is my friend who invited me to the party."

"Sasha's party?"

"No. I don't know whose party."

"So, what? You'll go with any boy who invites you to a party?"

"Sasha is a girl."

Her mother glared at her through the pass-through, her fingers curled around a naked white potato. "It's a *boy's* name. Short for Alexander."

Yaël had almost finished scraping all the sauce off her cutlet. "Not in Canada."

Her mother put the potato into the pot before she said, "What's it short for?"

Yaël thought of the tight complete tinyness that was Sasha. "That's all it is. Just Sasha."

"Who's Sasha?" That was Abey, just coming in from the hall.

"Sasha is Yaël's new friend that is taking her to a party."

"I'm taking myself. We're meeting there."

Her brother was wearing dusty coveralls and he didn't take them off before he sat down next to Yaël. She watched carefully to see if any dust was floating towards her robe. He narrowed his dark eyes. "Boy-Sasha or girl-Sasha?"

Yaël's kept her big blue eyes round. "Girl." She cut another piece of meat and chewed it at him. The sauce had soaked into the breading. She set her fork down and said, "Mama, I'm done. Want me to give the rest to Chien?"

"That's all you're eating? Wait a minute, I'll finish making Abey's potatoes and then you can have some, too. And don't feed it to Chien, the vet don't want him having scraps. He's been getting fat, old boy."

"I am not eating potatoes. And Chien is not fat. I gotta get my hair fixed."

Abey stretched out his legs so that Yaël had to walk around to put her plate on the counter. "Did they like the new logo?" he asked.

"Of course. They loved the whole presentation," she snapped, and went upstairs to finish herself.

*

There was a short in the hair dryer, so that it still worked but took twice as long to dry her hair, and left little waves behind her ears. Sasha had never once said anything about Yaël's hair, but then, men failed to mention, too – hair just went into the whole overall picture that they either did or did not like.

Then her last pair of good stockings snagged on the drawer so she had to wear the store-brand emergency pair, which puckered at the waist. By the time she got back downstairs, Yaël was in a mood, but her father was there so she had to be nice.

"Hey, Pop. How was your day?" She got her party boots from the closet and looked them over. She didn't have time for polish, but the burgundy leather looked glossy enough.

"Awight." Her father was eating, hunched over the table with his suit jacket on the back of his chair inside out. She waited for what her father would ask; her mother would have prepped him, like an executive for a meeting. He muttered through a spoonful of potatoes, "Them bosses like your logo idea?"

"Well, of course."

"Whose party you going to tonight?"

Yaël zipped a boot. "I don't know. It's my friend Sasha's friend."

"This is a girlfriend, your mother tells me. How do you know her?"

The boots looked good with a short skirt. She usually wore them with long skirts. "She was a temp at work."

Her father swallowed his mouthful and looked at her.

"A *temp*orary secretary. When someone was away last month."

"So she is a new friend. What about Lahley and Jane?"

"Tomorrow. We're going shopping." Yaël put her fingers to her lips to blow her father a kiss. When she held out her hand, she thought she saw a chip on her thumbnail polish, but it was just the light. Her mother came into the room dragging Chien by his leash. He did look a little plump. "Good night," said Yaël. "I'm going."

*

Yaël stopped at the LCBO. It was crowded, happy and loud, a miniature party made up of people from different parties, in ball caps and suits and dresses. Yaël stared the men in ties and jackets, the punker boys with gluey hair, the mousy girls in boring jeans. She stared at the rack of red wines and tried to imagine what Sasha's smart university friends would want. She decided the one that cost $15.

She parallel-parked the first try, but stayed in the car an extra moment to settle herself. If she were meeting a man at this party, her usual guy-from-work type from marketing or PR (she never dated corporate-branding guys; in-department dating was a mess), arriving would be the best part of the night. She tried to transpose all those past evenings into a new fantasy – Yaël coming in, getting hugged close to Sasha's small chest, getting introduced to impressed smiles, that first glass of wine of the weekend. She pulled back the handbrake and looked into the rearview. Her eyes were still perfect, all dark outline and silvery shadow. She got out of the car, clutching the wine bottle's throat through its paper sack.

She had never been to this neighbourhood before. The houses were big, but the lawns were patchy and no one had a flowerbed. Her boots rustled through leaves in the gutter. There were two guys sitting on the steps at the address Sasha had eyelinered on a sushi menu for her. Yaël was happy when they stopped talking to look at her boots, her breasts, her hair. Not the best part, but close. There were some pleasures in men, always.

"Is this the place where the party is?" She smiled at the boy on the left. His hair was feathery and too long around his face, but he had a nice big smile.

"Abso*lute*ly." He stood up and looked down at her open jacket, the clingy white angora sweater underneath, then at her face. "Welcome."

His friend stood up, too. "I'm Pete," he said, but he didn't extend a hand for her to shake. Neither of them did.

"I'm Yaël, Sasha's . . . Thanks for having me. I brought some wine." She held out the bottle, but Pete didn't take it.

"Oh, it's not my party. I'm just a friend of Hassid's. But I know there's a corkscrew in the kitchen for the wine. Oh, and this is Jarrit."

She turned. "Your party?"

"Oh, no. Those guys are inside."

Pete sat back down and picked up his beer. Jarrit smiled at her some more.

"Have you seen Sasha?"

His smile collapsed like a tent. "Oh, you're *with* Sasha? Oh. She was around before . . . I saw her."

Yaël was bored bored bored. She said, "Thanks," smiled nicely at Jarrit and carried the wine up the stairs and through the open front door. The party didn't seem to be in full swing yet. There were only a few people on the couches and they didn't look up when she came in. They all wore jeans, sweaters, sock feet. Some loopy music playing in the background, the same sample over and over. It was a little too warm. Yaël tucked the bottle between her knees and slid off her jacket.

A tall girl with a lot of toffee-coloured hair came running up. "Oh, wow, I just love those boots, those are gorgeous boots." The girl talked like a ring tone, but a compliment is a compliment, plus she took the bottle and pointed out the coatrack. When Yaël had hung up her coat she introduced herself and shook the girl's silky hand.

"I'm Bess," the girl said, handing the wine back. She wore no mascara, had bruisy bags under her eyes, a thin silver wire around the tip of one eyebrow.

"I'm Yaël." Yaël took the bottle reluctantly. "Nice place."

"Oh, I don't live here. I'm just a friend of Jarrit's. You meet Jarrit?"

"On the steps."

They stared at each other, blinking. Yaël couldn't imagine telling Bess about her beautiful logo swirl in pantone 292, glowingly approved by all senior management. Bess's chest was approximately 36C, in a tight white T-shirt that said in red letters, Vote for Pedro. She wondered if that was someone's first or last name.

Bess shifted from foot to foot. "I'm gonna go talk to Jarrit. There's a corkscrew in the kitchen, if you want. Sasha was in there before, making guacamole. You know Sasha? She makes awesome guacamole."

"Awesome," Yaël said faintly, and went on to the kitchen. The music was quieter there, but it was even warmer, and no Sasha. Someone saw Yaël's wine bottle and tried to give her a corkscrew; she flatly refused. Everybody stared at her, the everybody there was, which wasn't many. They weren't chatty, either, though few people had asked whether she was in the masters or doctoral stream, who her advisor was, who she TA'd for and what year she was in. Then Yaël didn't want to chat anymore – she didn't know what she was doing at this party anymore. She was the only one wearing shoes. She found a bathroom and locked herself in.

The sweat from her hand had soaked through the LCBO bag, so she took it off the bottle and threw it in the wastebasket. Then she hugged the wine to her chest and sat on the lid of the toilet until someone knocked on the door.

"Minute!" Yaël took out her cell and scrolled the numbers. While she was scrolling, it rang. "What?"

"Hey, so, you make it to the party ok?" Deep laughter in the background, the rustle of a crowd.

"Abey, I can drive a car." Someone tried the door. "Just a *minute!*"

"Yeah, but like, new place, new people." Beyond Abey was a sound like a foghorn.

"Are you at the game, Abey?"

"Yeah, but you need a ride, no problem, Yaël, I just had the one beer so far."

"Abey, I'm *fine.*" Yaël stared at the crumpled orange bath towel by the radiator. If Abey came and got her, he'd take her home if she wanted, but otherwise to the sports bar near the Allen, where she could order wine by the glass and not be responsible for the bottle, and every guy in the place would watch her and want her, but no one would talk to her because she was with Abey. It would be easy, and more fun then sitting on the toilet lid while her hair frizzed.

"This Sasha-friend, she's looking after you, I guess?"

"Abey, I'm fine, but there's so much static." There was no static, it was a very good cellphone and she kept it fully charged. "I gotta get off."

"Sure, but if ya – " Yaël hit End, then dialed.

Sasha picked up on the third ring, laughing, then, "Um, yeah? Hello?"

"Sasha? Are you there?" She stood up, peered into the mirror at her mouth.

"*Yaël.* Are you there?" There were men's voices in the background, and the same music that was coming through the bathroom door.

"I'm here." Yaël put the wine on the sink-edge, but it was curved and the bottle almost pitched before she caught it.

"Wait, *here* on the phone or *here* at the party? Where are you?"

"I'm here. I'm both. I'm in the bathroom." Yaël put the wine on the floor next to the plunger. It stayed there.

"You're here! That's so great. I was worried you wouldn't come. Someone said they saw you, but they said your hair was wavy. Did you do something new?"

Yaël pressed her hips against the edge of the vanity and leaned forward to look at herself in the three-way. The hot rooms had undone some of the straight-ironing. A thick blonde wave bumped either side of her jaw. Yaël pushed out a breath. "Where are you?"

"Laundry room. Behind the kitchen. Come right now. We have guacamole and chips. Well, we have chips."

"And beer!" someone yelled in the background.

Sasha laughed. "Come right now." Then dial tone.

Yaël put her phone back in her purse and took out her Almond Plum lipstick. She put some on almost carelessly, glaring at her hair. There was a big round brush on the back of the toilet. It took her a moment of thinking about germs before she picked it up. It took a much longer moment to pluck all the curly brown hair out of the bristles. The brushing didn't even do much good. Yaël set the brush back in its basket and started to look for a blow dryer, but then her purse rang. She gave up and opened the door.

There was a guy in the hall, leaning against the wall with his yellow Kodiaks crossed at the ankles, waiting patiently. He smiled when he saw her – at her face not her sweater, even – but she didn't feel up to another new person, so she kept going. At least there was someone else there wearing footwear.

Back in the kitchen, she found a door beside the refrigerator. Sasha was sitting on a shiny white drier, a brown beer bottle clutched to her thigh, her phone to her ear. She flipped it closed when Yaël came in. "You were taking too long. I've *missed* you." She hopped off the drier and stretched up to kiss Yaël on the mouth. Yaël felt herself blush before she could help it, but Sasha just hopped back on the drier and scooted over to make room.

Yaël licked Chapstick and beer that the kiss had left on her mouth, though she didn't like either taste. Then she examined the seating situation. Sasha was a good six inches shorter than her and she had been able to get easily from floor to drier, but Sasha was wearing purple skate shoes and jeans. Yaël was wearing a slim black skirt that stopped well above the knee, high boots and hose. She leaned against the drier instead, beside Sasha's legs but not touching. Sasha lowered her eyebrows, scooted closer and put an arm around Yaël's shoulder. Then she drank deeply from her beer, gestured across the room and said, "Yaël, this is Alan, and Sarah, and that's Cal."

"It's nice to meet you," Yaël said without moving. She had decided she didn't want to shake any more hands tonight. No one seemed offended.

The friend named Alan was sitting on top of the washing machine and did not notice he was being introduced. He wore a black wool peacoat, and was slouched so far forward his stomach touched his thighs. The girl, Sarah, was standing beside him and Alan was saying something in her ear, beneath her long frizzy hair. The hems of Sarah's jeans were salt-stained. In September. Cal was fiddling with a spinning-reel drying line mounted on the wall. All Yaël could see of him was a German army jacket and lank fair hair. Still facing away the wall, he said, "What kind of name is Yaël?"

"It's my name." Her parents were probably watching a movie right now, with pajamas and tea, probably something with Hugh Grant or Eddie Murphy falling down.

"It sort of rhymes with Cal. But not really. You sorta have two syllables." The clothesline suddenly whirled back into the reel. Cal jumped and finally turned. Yaël was surprised that he had a wide, handsome face and small fashionable glasses. He gestured with his beer. "My full name is Callum, rhymes with Alan. That's why we're roommates."

"That is not why we're roommates." Alan had been listening after all.

"That doesn't really rhyme, either. Al-*an*. Cal-*lum*." Yaël tried out the words like sour milk on her tongue. Sasha rubbed her shoulder.

"Not when you say it like that. It's slant rhyme, anyway." Cal moved towards her, gesturing with his beer bottle.

She straightened, re-centering herself over the heels of her boots. "What's slant rhyme?" The music in the other room was getting louder. She was thirsty, even though she hated the carb-y beer smell all around her. She actually really liked Hugh Grant.

"What?" Cal backed off, startled, and then jumped backward onto the washing machine. One of his elbows dug hard into Alan's belly, knocking him half to the floor, half onto Sarah. "You don't know what slant rhyme is? What are you *in*?"

Sarah pushed Alan upright. He tugged his coat and looked at Yaël expectantly. They all did, except Sasha who already knew and just petted Yaël's sweater like a kitten.

"I'm a brand manager for a family of lifestyle magazines," Yaël said slowly.

Cal flinched as if he had been struck. Alan whispered into Sarah's hair.

Sasha's voice shrilled. "Hey, you want a beer? Yaël? I'll bring you a beer. Better, I'll bring you *to* the beer, then you can choose. There's lots of kinds." Sasha slid down, gripped Yaël's shoulder, and pulled her to the kitchen.

"I don't like beer." Yaël was half-watching the strangers bickering by the stove, half-watching Sasha's pink T-shirt curve the faded words *Alpha Girl* across her chest. They stood close together. The kitchen was more crowded now.

"Oh, right, I forgot. I did know that, though." Colour was sliding towards the roots of Sasha's pulled-back hair. "Something else then. Wine? Maybe there's wine?"

"There's a bottle of wine in the bathroom," said a boy in a green fedora. "I don't know where the corkscrew is, though."

"I don't want wine." Yaël shook her head and the ends of her waves brushed Sasha's face. She could smell the beer in Sasha's bottle, in her mouth.

"I want you to have a good time."

"I'll have a good time. I'm having a good time. I only just got here."

"This isn't much of a party. Nothing but beer, no food but chips . . ."

"Somebody said you were making guacamole before."

Sasha wrinkled her small nose. "It came out weird. I think it was because the avocados were in Hassid's car all week." She seemed to be talking without listening to herself. She sipped her drink, kicked her toes against Yaël's, put her free hand on her hip, then on Yaël's hip, squeezed. Yaël squirmed, wishing she'd worn better stockings, and Sasha put her hand in her own pocket. "It's in the fridge, though. I'll get it." She turned.

"No, thanks." Yaël reached out and touched the overwashed cotton of Sasha's T-shirt shoulder. Sasha startled and turned back just as the guy in Kodiaks tried to pass between them. He kicked hard into Sasha's ankle, and Sasha jolted, her arms flailing out for balance. A foamy spurt of her beer jumped across the air and onto Yaël's thin white angora, soaking her sheer peach bra quickly, cold against her hot right breast.

"Oh, shit, sorry," the guy muttered and walked on without looking at the girls, the sweater, Sasha's bloodred face.

"Oh, shit, sorry," said Sasha, staring at Yaël's wet and yellowed and half-translucent and very expensive sweater. "I am so sorry. I really – "

Yaël put her mouth down on Sasha's hairline, where blush met blonde. She knew Sasha would never have makeup on her forehead, or product in her hair. She ran her tongue slowly along Sasha's temple, felt the texture of skin, tasted the tang of sweat, heard the silence between songs in the CD changer.

To: All onsite employees
From: Building Services
Re: Monthly Fridge Cleanup

Wednesday 10:19 a.m.

Dear Dream Team,

Please note that this Friday evening is our monthly fridge cleanup. Please be aware that any food items that you wish to keep must NOT be left in any Dream Inc. office kitchen over the weekend. The cleaning staff does not have time to assess everything in the fridge – if it is left this Friday evening, it will be considered abandoned.

Please evaluate and collect your food stores accordingly. Happy snacking!
Gregster

AFTER THE MEETING

AFTER THE MEETING WAS OVER, we got in Wayne's car, since he was the only one who had a car, and started driving back into town. We figured we'd go to Martin's, but on the way we picked up a two-four, a pizza, and a box of Jos Louis. Since we were all unemployed now, the beer was domestic and the pizza was from this Iranian place by the highway, but I wouldn't compromise on the Jos Louis.

"Metro brand is shit," I told Danvir. He shrugged, but I could tell he agreed.

As we walked down the alley to the basement, Martin said, "They shoulda let us take our stuff, like the stuff from our desks. They shouldn't have made us go straight-aways, 'cause it'll suck to take all that on the bus if Wayne's not there."

"And I *won't* be there, man – all I got in that desk is the manual and some Craisins."

"Mmm, Craisins," is what I said, because I had skipped breakfast thinking I'd get a muffin from the caf to eat at my desk while I worked, only there was no work that morning, because we were busy getting laid off.

Martin's place was big, sort of, but with everything around a corner from everything else, and these pillars spiking up at random, so the chesterfield, TV, and chairs were all sort of huddled up in front of the kitchen. Plus the rubber underneath the carpet had dried up so it crackled when you walked. There was cat hair on everything, white and light like dandelion fluff, but I didn't see any actual cats.

It wasn't until Wayne had tipped his big ass onto the chesterfield and opened up the pizza box on his knees that anyone talked about what had actually happened.

"Well, fuck." That was Martin, but he'd swear at a baby.

It was sadder to hear Danvir say it. "Fuck, indeed. The caterers' payment is due next month. Ally's gonna divorce me 'fore we're even married."

Wayne had a faceful of pizza but he still muttered, "Wait'll Kayly gets the news; then we'll have fuck."

Martin just sighed, maybe because gay boyfriends don't yell at each other, I dunno.

I was single, so all I said was "I wish I hadn't had that stupid fight with my mom, 'cause now I can't go stay with her if I can't make rent."

Danvir bugged out his eyes at the same time as he reached for my Jos Louis box. "You got *some* savings, right, Will? You're not gonna be totally broke in two weeks, right?"

I watched him take one out. "I got expenses, man. And two-weeks notice is sorta dick-all – I'm not gonna get a job in two weeks."

I had the one chair and Danvir had the other, and Wayne had most of the chesterfield. Martin was skinny and could have fit in beside him, but he was just hovering around, making the carpet crackle. For a gay, he sure was skittish about touching a man. Finally he sort of slouched one cheek down on the arm of the thing, and said, "It *is* terrible, though – two weeks after, how long? I've been there almost three years, I think. God, is that possible?"

"Ah, don't go there, all them wasted years," Danvir said.

I was still working on the plastic wrap to get at my snack cake, mainly because I was distracted by thinking so hard. Finally I tore it open at the same moment I worked out what I wanted to say. "What I don't get is what we did wrong? Mark and Sanjeet shoulda said. Cause I thought the call-completion times, the renewal rates, well, we were pretty badass, weren't we?"

Danvir shook his head. "Too soon for *were*, Will. Say *are* for a bit, still."

Wayne finally swallowed and looked serious. "We didn't do anything wrong, kid, don't you worry about that. What we didn't do was work for a dollar a day. You couldn't have beat those sweatshops in Delhi or somewhere, no matter what yer close rate."

My Jos Louis got away from me before I'd got to take even one bite. Everyone watched it somersault under the coffee table. I looked up at Martin. "Would you eat that?"

"Probably not. Not with the cats."

"Cats?" Danvir stood half-way up and looked around. "I hate cats."

I got down on my knees and grabbed the cake. There weren't any obvious hairs on it, and the chocolate coating hadn't cracked. There were only six in the box, and I had $117 in the bank. I nibbled a little chocolate off and said, "What'd a cat ever do to you?"

Wayne was still on the other thing. "*Offshore vendors* – " he made air quotes with his greasy fingers " – a bunch of starving kids with flies on them chained to desks to punch in *Dream Sailing* subscription orders."

Martin opened his mouth and eyes wide and flapped his hands at Wayne. "C'mon, be a little sensitive." He jerked his ear at Danvir.

And then Danvir dropped his Jos Louis – it was an epidemic. At least his was still wrapped. But he didn't even bend for it, just glared at Wayne and Martin. "Fuck you. I'm from Scarborough."

"Yeah, but like . . ." Martin jumped upright, waving his beer. I wanted a beer. ". . . your parents?"

Danvir stood up, too. He stepped on the Jos Louis and I heard the bag pop. "They run a car lot on Ellesmere – they don't want your job."

"Wait," I said suddenly. "If they're just sending the *Dream Sailing* orders over there, why'd they lay off *all* of us?"

Wayne rolled his eyes. "It was a general statement. They're sending it all, so you can order your *Dream Wedding, Dream Baby,* whatever subscriptions in Hindi now too."

"People speak English there."

"But I mean, now, Hindi's an option."

"That's what you meant? Really?"

I started chewing, tasting carefully, chocolate and cream. It didn't taste like cat, so I took another bite. I always eat when I'm stressed out, just like my mom. Maybe we could live together again, if I apologized.

"What do you *think* I mean? Speak your mind, Danvir – you got a problem with me?" Martin was maybe 140 with his clothes on, but the thing was, so was Danvir – so was I, for that matter. Most of the guys in customer service were not setting the world on fire, tough-guy-wise. Or anything-wise. Except Wayne, with his knees the size of basketballs and head two feet above the top of the couch. If there was a scrap, and suddenly it felt like there might be, everyone but Wayne was pretty even money.

"I think you're racist, is what I think."

Martin bumped down on the chesterfield next to Wayne. "Racist? *I'm* racist? Wayne is practically my best friend and he's *black* and *I'm* racist?"

Wayne looked down at Martin as if from on top of a mountain, but Danvir jumped in first. "Not like that, not like . . . skin, just skin . . ." He was pacing, furious, his tear-away basketball pants rasping as he walked. "Wayne's as Canadian as you are, so what's the difference? That's what you think, you think, right, you two are the insiders with no accent, no immigration papers."

Wayne swallowed hard on a ball of pizza and looked like he was thinking about standing up too. "My great-gramma came from Jamaica in 1942."

"You are – you think *I'm* not out a job, same as you, 'cause my ma's got a sari in the back of her closet?"

"It isn't about hating on you, or your ma. It's just about, you know, why they gotta take the jobs outta Canada and – "

"That's where your thinking is totally fucked. I mean, fucked." Danvir suddenly crouched down to look in the two-four beside his chair, like there were a bunch of different options in there and he was choosing very carefully. "Like them Indian call-centre jerks – like they come with guns and make Dream Inc. shift the inbound call operations to India."

Wayne nodded slowly. "He's right, the fucker. They ain't taking what Mark and Sanjeet doan wanna give."

"Hey, *Sanjeet* . . . doesn't sound like a name of someone who wants Canadians – "

"Oh, shut *up,* Martin. Who'da thought *you'd* be the racist one?" Danvir kinda cackled and popped his beer.

"I *ain't* the racist one." Martin chewed.

Danvir slurped then chewed.

I noticed a guy who looked like the WWF come through the kitchen behind the couch where everybody else was eating and drinking and yelling.

"Why *wouldn't* I be the racist one, anyway? What kind of thing is that to say?"

It was, seriously, the muscliest guy I'd ever seen. His shirt wasn't even that tight and there wasn't much light in the kitchen, but I could see bulges in his shoulders, bulges in his chest, and his hair was shaved off so his head was like one giant shiny bulge.

"I dunno – " Danvir was being all fake, like he does when he knows he's right on trivia night " – you bein' a homosexual, I though you mighta learned a little tolerance."

The guy in the kitchen put his hands on his waist and I saw it was really narrow, his top half actually triangling down into his pants. I thought about how I ought to join a gym a second before I remembered that I was unemployed.

Some food fell out of Wayne's mouth. I was only just now realizing how bad the light was in there as I tried to see if it was Jos Louis or pizza and I couldn't. Wayne turned and looked at Martin for a good long second, food still sitting on his shirt like a Remembrance Day poppy. "Yer a fag?"

Danvir hooted like he'd just bowled a strike. "*Practically best friends,* huh?"

The guy took a step into the living-room light, and I could see that he wasn't black, though he wasn't exactly white, either.

Martin flopped along the back of the couch until he was all the way lying down and Wayne had to squirm around to look at him, which knocked the pizza box to the floor. The pizza mainly stayed in even though the box didn't shut all the way.

"You are a *faggot?*"

The kitchen guy took another step.

"You knew that." Martin tossed his hands in the air and then flopped them back on his belly. "Everybody knows that. How could you not know that?"

Wayne was twisting around to kneel backwards on the couch, no easy game for a guy his size. "*I* didn't know cuz *you* din't tell me. You don't say, Wayne, I am a homosexual, you don't try to make sweet love to me when I drop a pencil, I don't know you are gay. Simple."

"I am glad," said the man, stepping fully into the room and putting a hand on Martin's chest, "that you do not try to make love to strangers when they drop pencils."

Martin jumped about a mile when the guy touched him, but he somehow managed not to fall off the couch. The guy didn't sound like a wrestler. He had an English accent and sounded like he should've been on TV explaining how an amoeba works.

"They aren't strangers, Lee," Martin said, struggling to sit up without falling onto Wayne. "These guys are from Dream."

"We're all *best* friends," said Danvir, who had sat back down in his chair again. His voice was supposed to sound like he was trying not to laugh, I guess, but it didn't really sound like he found much funny at all.

Wayne twisted back around and looked into space, only it was the space where I was sitting.

Martin stood up finally, next to Lee, also facing me but not really looking.

"So these are the people you work with," said Lee very quietly.

"Yep, work with. Really not friends at all."

There was more silence then, all of us just looking and thinking and breathing in pizza air. All those eyes on me, everyone so angry, and yet the day before, playing Hackey-Sack in the kitchen with that balled-up invoice, making fun of Patty Jacobson for calling Levis *designer jeans*, even just an hour ago talking about how the Iranian pizza place was ok and the Halal pepperoni was awesome. And then I realized it was over.

"No, we don't work together anymore," I said. "That's all done with now."

BURSTING INTO
TEARS EVERY
TWENTY MINUTES

ON TUESDAY MORNING, Sarah kept her face under the itchy afghan long after the alarm had gone off, watching sunlight filter through the loops of pink and orange wool. She was drenched in sweat. Only when the phone rang and her mother shrieked, "*Sarah!*" did she pull her head out. The air in the room felt cool in her wet hair.

"Phone, Sarah! I mean it."

The beige cordless on the nightstand was smudged with grey. "You up?"

"I'm up, yeah. What?" The bedside clock said eight-eleven, too late for a shower.

"I'm making sure you're up, Sar. If you're late again, Kief's gonna fuckin' make you into gravy."

"I won't be late. I'm up." Sarah scissor-kicked the blankets onto the floor, covering the clean laundry, the lamp, her grade 11 biology text.

"How are our fertile friends?"

"I don't know. She's still here, that's it." She swung her legs over and sat up. Her head felt hot and heavy, filled with melted candlewax.

"Ok, one problem at a time. Get moving. You should be on the bus already." There was a click, a moan of dial tone.

Sarah was tempted to put her uniform on over her T-shirt and shorts, to avoid being naked, but people – at least Kate – would notice the lumps under her chef's jacket and white-and-black checked pants. She stripped down to her panties and bra, then dressed, shivering.

Everyone was at the kitchen table for some reason, drinking tea and eating whole-wheat bread out of the silver Wonder sack. Jeremy was reading job ads aloud in a voice like Jerry Seinfeld's, only not funny, and Margaret was retching quietly into an HMV bag. Sarah's mom sat blinking at the wall, drinking her tea. Her mother had to be at work at nine, too. "Who was on the phone?"

". . . to transit freight to and from stations and hub facilities, as well as pickup and delivery of skidded freight . . . What, *skidded*, like, slipped?"

"It means on skids, those wooden flats that hold freight, Jeremy," their mother said, then took a sip of tea. "Sarah, you gonna eat?"

Jeremy muttered through crumbs, "I . . . I guess I could do that. You don't have to lift them yourself, right? They let you use a . . . a . . ."

Margaret coughed, then spat.

"No." Sarah sat down on the bench beside the door to do up her sneakers. They had once been white, but now they were gravy-coloured. "Just Kate."

"At this hour?" Her mother reached into the bag. "Forklift, probably." She handed a slice of bread to Sarah. It crumpled in her hand like a Kleenex.

"Good morning, Sarah," Margaret said in a wavering voice. "I – I'm sorry, sorry, about all this."

Jeremy put the paper down and patted Margaret's knee without looking at her. "Yeah, morning, Sar."

Margaret looked so pathetic, sad and fat and clutching her sack of vomit, Sarah couldn't even answer.

Margaret wiped her mouth and tried to smile, but it went wobbly straightaway. Jeremy kept looking at the paper. Sarah's mother raised her mug and tipped it against her lips before realizing it was empty. Sarah squashed the damp bread in her palm and fled.

Sarah had never seen Margaret's parents' house, but she was sure it had a lawn, two stories, shutters and eavestroughs painted to match. She was sure Margaret's family didn't eat dry bread for breakfast, not even the week before payday. When Margaret started dating Jeremy, she would tell Sarah about horses and manicures, and Sarah was happy enough to nod and smile and imagine. Now that Margaret had gotten pregnant and kicked out, nobody really talked to her anymore, barely even Jeremy.

*

Two blocks hot walk to the bus stop and a half-hour's ride west, until the roadside was mainly blank and the bus almost empty. The back of the cafeteria was still under construction though the place had been open a month. Staff had to pick their way through mud to the door, then down the long employees-only corridor where the lights were always shorting out. Between the walk-in fridge and freezer were the punch clock and a mirror hanging from a nail. Sarah stopped there, took a hairnet from her back pocket and started trying to push her hair in. She had a lot, and every time she seemed to get a good bunch in, she'd go to tuck in the last couple curls, and the whole fro would spring back out again. She could feel tears starting her throat.

"If you won't shave it, at least put it up in a bun. This is torture."

Everything startled Sarah, but not Kate's voice. "I don't have the skull shape. I wouldn't look like you. I would look like a tall toddler."

"Only hotter," Kate said reflexively. It was what she always said when Sarah made fun of herself. "How you doing?"

"Oh, you know, bursting into tears every twenty minutes. You?"

Kate did look good, all cheekbone and jaw, just fuzz on her skull. She punched herself In, then Sarah.

"I'm not ready." Sarah turned and more hair tumbled free. "Leave it."

"Keif just notices what's on the card, not what you actually do. You gotta be on time on paper."

"That's lying." Sarah's voice was thin; she found it hard to even hear herself over the hum of the fridge and freezer. The hairnet slipped out of her hands, onto the onion-skin-strewn floor.

Kate sighed so deeply her belly puffed under the chef shirt. "C'mere, I'll do it."

Sarah scrabbled on the floor. "I can do it, I just need – "

Kate snatched the net and shook off the gunge with one hand. With the other, she took Sarah's hair and twisted it roughly into a bun. A few strands stretched, broke, but Sarah didn't say anything. The hairnet went on smoothly, more or less. Kate tapped Sarah on her spine. "You're done. You're on the clock. Get to work."

*

Breakfast sandwiches sold out early, and the customers stuck with toast and jam grumbled. Then a coffee urn jammed, which meant it had to be dumped out and the valve dismantled. Plus Sarah and Kate had to make deli trays for lunch meetings, rolling glistening pink ham and white-freckled salami into cylinders.

It was 11:00 before Sarah could start on lunch specials. Kate was on ketchups, but after Sarah had only produced six chicken-avocado wraps in twenty minutes, Kief said condiments were less important than the food people paid for, and sent Kate to help.

"You're pissing him off, Sar. Next time, warn me you're fucking up so I can help *before* he sees. You know? Cause you're pissing him off."

"I know. I gotta get my head in the game." A piece of avocado squirted out the end of a wrap.

"You sound like Jeremy. You been talking to Jeremy?"

"Uh . . . no, not really."

"Did you even ask how far along she is?" Kate dotted avocado pieces down the middle of a spinach tortilla.

"*How far along?* You sound like somebody's great aunt."

"Riiightt . . . ok, but did you? Cause if she's gonna end it she's gotta do it before like, three months or something."

"End it. Yeah. I dunno." Kate's sandwich was a smooth green phallus while Sarah's was lumpy and leaking salsa. "I don't think me asking will decide much."

"The whole situation is so fucked up. It sounds like no one's deciding."

Sarah couldn't picture the abortion or the birth. Either way, a white hospital room: Margaret pale and serious under a sheet getting a whole other life pulled out of her. And now Margaret was drained of her powers, her straight-A grades and her smiles, her *Glamour* dog-eared to haircuts she thought might look good on her friends, even her ability to keep down her breakfast.

The next wrap rolled more smoothly, but then Sarah realized she hadn't tucked the ends in and had to undo it. "Shit."

"Chill. We got a little time until lunch rush."

A small gravelly throat-clear made them turn. A woman with a sharp bob and shiny silver glasses was standing beyond the stainless steel counter. Sarah kept Saran-wrapping her deformed wrap until the thing was a baton of shimmering silver. Kate would, she knew, eventually go deal with the woman. Except then Kief yelled from somewhere, "Katy, you gonna take out this garbage or are we gettin' a health violation?"

Kate jerked her gloves off by the fingers. "*Katy*. Vomit." She stormed away.

"Excuse me? Hi? I need a turkey and cheese on honey wheat? Toasted."

Sarah's hands shook as she peeled off her gloves. Non-specials were actually much harder than specials. She stuck slices of gritty bread into the toaster, wondering what she'd done with the piece her mother gave her. She got a plate and the corn chips.

The customer had been glaring at her Blackberry until she heard the crinkle of the Tostitos bag; then her eyes rounded childishly. "Oooo, chips!" The tiny screen buzzed in her hand.

Only a few chip-triangles fell onto the plate, plus crumbs. Sarah searched for a new bag until the toaster pinged. When she applied the chicken the woman thumbed her keypad and said, "Sliced thinly, please," without looking up.

"Uh." Sarah flapped a chicken slice. "It comes in the package, just the one thickness, er, thinness. I don't know how to get it thinner than this. I mean . . ."

"Oh." The woman flushed behind her glasses. "Of course not. I was thinking of the deli. Of course, of course." Sarah put the chicken in the bread, watching the woman rummage her tweed torso for something. They had reached the optional-toppings stage but the woman was muttering into her phone – "not Sunday, *Mon*day."

Finally, after waving each garnish in turn (drops of brine flying off the pickle slices), watching for the nod or shake, Sarah finished the sandwich. Kief was bumping around in the back as if he was monitoring her. She passed the sandwich over the counter.

"Thanks."

A man in a blue shirt gift-wrap tight over his belly approached.

"Can I help who's next?" Sarah said, though it was clear who was next.

"Yeah, uh, I'll get the, uh, egg salad – "

"Excuse me, miss?" The woman had returned, mouth a tight bow.

The man kept ordering his *pickles, no onions,* and Sarah listened, feeling it safer.

"I said, *excuse* me, *miss!*"

"I'm sorry, sir, one moment. Yes?"

Suddenly the woman flinched, as if she hadn't thought Sarah would actually turn. "I don't mean to be . . . I'm – There aren't enough chips here. And they're all smushed."

"There are chips." She pointed at the woman's plate.

"Um," said the woman. "Like four."

The egg-salad guy and the woman were both glaring. Sarah managed to reach across the counter. But the woman didn't hand over the plate, using it instead to gesture at someone. "*She* has twice as many chips as me. And she's *already eaten some.*"

Sarah realized that she hadn't said, *I'd be happy to get you some more,* only thought it. She took her hand back; she couldn't say anything now because tears were haloing the light in the caf, a sob in the back of her throat.

The woman was staring. "Are you . . . ok?"

Sarah only got as far as "I – " and even that was obscured by a hiccup. A tear escaped her left eye, but when it was passing her nose she inhaled hard and slurped it in.

"Hey, never mind. I was just being silly." But the woman was still there, still staring, so she still wanted something.

Sarah reached mutely for the plate, but the trimmed, no-polish hand pulled it back. "Should I get someone?"

The thought of Kief – his curls plastered to his forehead, his polo-shirt damp, face flushed with irritation – was too much. Sarah fled.

Her pants already had avocado and jam on them, so it didn't matter that she sat on the bathroom floor. It was dirty, but she didn't think any of her fellow employees would actually piss on the floor. After about ten minutes sitting under the paper-towel dispenser, Sarah got her breathing under control, though she knew she wouldn't have been able to speak quite normally. She wondered if anyone noticed her absence, and then realized the woman with insufficient chips had probably told Kief everything. She knew she should go out to apologize, to show Kief, the bob-haired lady, and Kate that she was all right.

Thinking about Kate was what made Sarah tip sideways until her head rested against the base of the toilet and her left shoulder blade in something wet. Yet Sarah half-wished for Kate's inevitable knock. She was hoping, a little, that Kate's clean common sense could jog her loose from whatever held her to the floor, whatever held her mother to boiled noodles and non-complaint, the whole household dusty and grey, with mold behind the bookcase. Sarah and Kate had been friends since kindergarten and Kate had never understood, but sometimes she could help anyway.

And there was that firm voice from beyond the door. "Sarah?"

Sarah lay still and spooked, as if she had summoned her.

"It's *Kate*, Sarah. Kief's doing orders with the greengrocer guy. Lunch is *over.*"

Shocked that she'd wept or slept through the whole lunch rush, Sarah stood and opened the door.

Kate inhaled as if she were about to blow up a balloon. "What happened? What did that lady say to you? After you went, she looked like she was going to cry, too."

Sarah slurped snot up her nose and tried to breathe evenly. She stared at the domed ceiling light – dozens of dead flies in the nipple of it. When she turned back to Kate, Kate's small blue eyes were trained right on Sarah's forehead, like gun sights.

"Is the reason I haven't been fired yet is that Kief is scared of the ladies room?"

Kate flinched and peered more deeply at Sarah's face. Then she abruptly sat down, legs accordionning her onto the floor. "If you have a good excuse, like the customer was a giant bitch, you won't get fired."

"I – No. She was average. I just had a meltdown, is all." The words after *average* were watery, breathless. She lay down again, limp, beside Kate.

Kate's eyes narrowed even more, pale slits with the light of the fluorescent tube reflecting in them. "Can't you just . . . just . . . get it together?"

Sarah tried for another deep breath but there was the weight of a sob resting on her lungs and she didn't get much. "No."

Kate's eyes were motherly and bright, unlike Sarah's blank, exhausted mother. "Of course you can. It's like at school – English is hard so you study more, lacrosse is hard so you train more . . . . We'll, like, practice and shit. I'll be the mean customer and – "

"No, Kate, I can't."

"We'll do it at my dad's, Sary, I know things are fucked at your place right now. It'll be fun – we can drink the beers in the garage – he forgot they're there."

"Kate, it's like – " Sarah thought about how she couldn't tell Margaret that it was appalling to puke in the kitchen, even if you did use a bag and not get it anywhere else. She thought about how no one in her family could say that out loud, and that was why Margaret would have that baby: because no one could take that cruel decisive action to rip it out of her belly and send her back to school and horseback riding and real life. Sarah suddenly saw every test she never studied for because she needed to lie on her back and count ceiling cracks, and Jeremy dropping out of school for that catering job and the break in her mother's voice when she announced everyday sadness like bills in the mail or running out of salt.

She shut her eyes against the hot white light and the nipple of bugs. "It's not the job. Practicing work won't help. It's me."

"Keif is gonna be here in a minute, Sar. What are you gonna tell him?"

Kate was her best friend, and they had done everything together, Kate and Sarah, Sarah and Kate, kindergarten to grade 12, next year. So long trying to run faster, not cry when she fell, be smarter, not cry when she failed, get the boys to like her, not cry not cry not cry. Kate always wanting her to be better, more, different from how she was. It was a relief to think she would stop all that now, stop trying. But opening her eyes to look at Kate's hopeful smile and shiny skull, it was so hard to think how to tell her.

CHEESE-EATERS

9:12 a.m., Tuesday. Rae was slouched so far forward her breasts weighed on the desk. The optical mouse had fallen and disappeared, so she was using the trackball one. On the desk: one apple cut into eighths, one Chinese New Year prosperity fish, 34 overstuffed folders abandoned when Amelia went on disability, notepad, Kleenex box, water glass, and a small, limp fern. Under the desk: a silver cellphone and charger, wastepaper basket, three pairs of dark pumps, optical mouse, somewhere. It was the first day of the second month of her trial separation, which Rae was marking by wearing her wedding ring on a chain behind her blouse.

"Rae." Hamid stood in the opening between the grey baffle-cloth walls. His grey golf shirt hung free from his shoulders to his belt. Only his elbows and knees bulged; Hamid was all joints. "*Rae.*"

"Yes, Hamid." She did not lift her chest, or turn, or cease scrolling down.

"Ursula hired someone."

The trackball stuck. Rae was going to have to move the desk.

"And not admin. A junior designer, for real."

"Amazing." She clicked save twice, then finally turned. She could feel the necklace shift. "When do we get it?"

Hamid raised his left elbow above his head, pushing it down with his right hand to stretch his triceps. "Her. Today. Now."

"Today? I don't have time for a welcome lunch. Ursula should've warned us."

"Ursula's off-site today." He shook his arms out. "Remember?"

"No. So? This person is here?"

"Sitting in HR, waiting for her tour."

"And you're gonna?"

"The hell I am. Hear about the marketing feedback on the new feature template? Looks like it's been mauled by sharks." Hamid bug-eyed her. He was older than she was, but lived with his parents, played indoor soccer, drove an ugly expensive car. He worked seventy hours a week, on salary.

"Hey, they don't like my column design, either."

"Raeanne, sharks. The branding division'll have my ass."

"Fine," said Rae, the way she would give up and let Marley and Jake have cookies. She stood and tugged her skirt down. The waistband was high and thick, digging in. "You gonna introduce me?"

Hamid was already three steps towards his cube. "I didn't see her, HR just called. Look for the scared one."

Rae thought about yelling, "We're all scared, Hamid," but didn't.

*

The girl wore a white eyelet blouse with ruffled cap sleeves, her left bra-strap visible. Pink. She nodded as Rae approached. The nod turned her messy chignon into a ponytail. Rae stuck out her hand and said, "Junior design?"

She got a beam in response. "Hello, hi. I'm Andrea Goss. Andy. I'm so glad to meet you, glad to be getting started here. Hi." At her feet a blue rain jacket, a Burberry lunch sack, a black leather shoulder bag the size of a Labrador retriever.

"I'm one of the senior designers, Raeanne." Andy had scooped everything from the floor and arranged it in her arms before Rae added, "Rae."

*

They saw the coffee room, the ladies room, the copier and the fax machine. ("No one will fax you. It's two thousand and *eleven*.") The big boardroom, the little boardroom, the dieffenbachia that hadn't died. Then the design room – four bus-shelter-sized file cabinets, twenty desks, a hibiscus with huge powdery red stamens.

"And this is my desk." Rae looked at her cosmos screensaver, her browning apple. Her pictures of her kids were in her purse; anyone could have sat at this desk. This desk was all she wanted.

"Where do *I* sit?"

Rae only knew all cubes on the window row were occupied: hers, Hamid's, Amelia who had bone cancer, weird silent Mallick, Andrew who sometimes whistled. There were empty cubes in the dark inner rows.

Rae fidgeted. Her phone rang, but she couldn't think how to answer politely. Someone was walking past, and she turned, hopeful. He was tall, from Tech – she couldn't remember his first name. "Luddock!"

"What can I do for you, Raeanne?" The Tech guys always knew your name, and probably everything about you, too.

"Have you set up a Mac for a new designer named Andrea . . . um . . ."

"Goss!"

"Of course." Luddock straightened, an insulted bird. "Something not working?"

"No, no, just . . . where is it?"

Luddock led them to an empty cube in the midst of empty cubes. "Here ya go!"

Rae had remembered that his first name was Arthur, but it seemed awkward to call him that now. "Thanks, Luddock."

Andy was looking at the fire regulations pinned to her baffle. "It's awfully far from yours. For, like, asking questions."

Rae was about to say Ursula would come back and answer questions, that Rae herself was not responsible for questions. Then Luddock pointed at the inner wall.

"Not far at all. Right next door. Just sit still and ask. She'll hear you." Luddock winked, and disappeared down the aisle.

Andy dropped all her things and opened the cupboard. "Lots of Quark manuals."

"Don't worry, we don't really use a lot of the weird features here."

"Weird features? I've not worked with it at all really."

"Oh."

Rae left her reading the first page of the manufacturer's guide. Without Quark, the job pretty much didn't exist.

When she got to her desk, Rae had 19 emails. She didn't touch her voicemail.

*

12:55. Rae was re-ordering Mallick's list of corrupted files, missing her good mouse. A rustle, then: "Rae? Um, for lunch? Is there a caf?"

"A lunchroom."

She could *see* the mouse, wedged between wall and desk. She just couldn't reach it. "Down in the basement."

"Oh, good."

"Not really." Rae kicked off her left shoe, stretched her foot up under the desk.

"I don't mind. I brought a sandwich."

"It's the . . . atmosphere."

"I have a spot." Hamid's voice over the wall. "And I can spare fifteen. Then I gotta razor this frickin' sailing spread."

Rae felt her nylon snag under the desk. "Andy, this is Hamid. He does our more complex Photoshop stuff."

"That's cool. I used Photoshop once, to make a collage of wedding cakes."

Rae stuffed her foot into her shoe. "Have a good lunch, guys." She touched her spacebar and the cosmos dispersed.

Andy's voice: "Couldn't we just . . . all go together?"

Rae thought about the blaze-red voicemail light, Amelia's unsorted files. She also thought about the meals she ate alone — most of them now. Every weeknight she put everything from the pot or pan or takeout tub onto her own plate. Every weekday she ate all the toast that popped out of the toaster. When the children came on Saturday, she was weakened to the point of pizza out of the box, red Gatorade, ice cream, all in front of the TV. "Give me a few minutes. I'll come."

*

It was more than an hour before Rae could log out. She took a fork from her *F* folder, went to Hamid's cube, and muttered, "Lunch!"

"She used Photoshop *once*? You better show her some tutorials," he whispered.

"I am *not* training her. That's not my job."

"Just today."

"No. They imprint, like baby geese. Scared new juniors, you show them how to do one thing, they think you're their mother, follow you around. I don't have time."

"That's a fascinating theory, Rae."

That's how it was with you was another thing she thought to say but didn't.

In Andy's cube, all the Quark manuals were open, bathed in the glow of a fishbowl screensaver. Andy knelt on the desk tacking up photos of a blond boy on skis.

"How's it going?"

Andy twisted. Her hair was down now. "This is my boyfriend? Topher?"

"Tomorrow Ursula will be here. She'll give you . . . something to do."

"I'm looking forward to it. Topher skis competitively? And he works in a bank?"

"Right. You want to go for lunch now?"

"Sure." Andy slid off the desk.

Rae turned towards the kitchen. She didn't check to see if Andy followed. She heard what was probably her own phone ringing. Her ring on its chain bounced hard off her sternum, catching the inside of her buttons.

Hamid came and led them to the fridge, then the stairs, the fire door. It was hot outside. They started across the parking lot.

"So, wedding cakes," Hamid said.

"I like wedding cakes."

"Difficult to light molded sugar. Very matte, and then glitter, like stones. Weird."

Rae's left heel skidded on the gritty asphalt.

Andy said, "I can hear . . . construction?"

"Demolition. They're knocking down a parking garage. You get used to it. We did. And Mallick never heard anything to start with."

"How long will it last? Who's Mallick?"

"October, supposedly. We'll see. Mallick sits behind me, mainly does text." Rae and Hamid had been answering the questions in alternation, walking single file across the wide silent asphalt. It didn't matter who answered; anyone who had been there more than a year shared the same body of knowledge and complaint.

They reached a thin strip of concrete edging a thin strip of grass edging a thin veil of trees edging the highway. Hamid sat down on the concrete lip. Rae sighed. She'd suspected something like this. She put her salad on the ground and began tucking her skirt in between her thighs. Clenching violently, she sat, knees at nipple level.

Andy's skirt was long and floaty, so she sat more easily, spread her knees to make a hammock for her sandwich. Hamid sprawled half on concrete, half on grass and tried to bite through a pizza pop wrapper.

"Are there any *so*cial things here?"

Rae picked up her Tupperware of spinach and diced ham. "What do you mean?"

"Like, my sister's on the social committee at her hospital? They went golfing?"

"I don't think . . . We're not the best people to ask."

Hamid was tossing the pop in the air between bites. "I'm pretty sure there's charity stuff. There's pictures of a dirty little orphan up in the lunchroom, with a mayonnaise jar full of loonies under it. Are you married? Engaged?"

"What? Me?" Andy's sandwich was pink ham and yellow mustard, white bread. Rae could see a Dad's Oatmeal Cookie packet in her bag. "No, I have a boyfriend, Topher. He works in a bank, and skis – "

Hamid waved his juice box. "Wedding cakes, I mean. Are you getting one?"

"Not yet." Andy shrugged a demure, inward shrug. "Maybe someday. You?"

"I might not be the marrying kind, I dunno. But maybe someday."

Rae had known Hamid for three years, and only ever seen him with colleagues. She had no idea if there was anyone specific he wasn't marrying. Which was a relief, since it meant he probably hadn't noticed that she wore a wedding band, then didn't.

"Oh, damn." She pointed at the run in her nylons she'd already known was there.

It had the desired effect, a switch in conversation. Andy didn't like nylons. Neither did Hamid. They both said why, in detail. Rae nodded thoughtfully.

Rae and Theo's wedding cake had been very plain, except for a dozen lavender sugar flowers with foil stamens that you couldn't eat. On their first anniversary, the thawed top layer had been surprising tasty, but ugly, the flowers all melted and deformed.

Andy's sandwich was just a crescent of crust. Soon they could go back in. Rae tried to judge the weight of Hamid's drinking box by the way he held it.

A Hummer blew by, enveloping them in grit and the thump of speakers. Probably a finance intern. Rae put the lid on her sandy half-eaten salad and stood, ready for the conversation, lunch, day to be over.

Andy scrambled up. "I had to park outside today. Do you think I can get an indoor pass?"

"I don't know." Rae started walking towards the building, and the others fell in step beside her. She hadn't had this much eye-contact with Hamid all year.

Andy was scanning the lot. "Where do you park?"

"I don't have a car right now."

Andy's lower lip dropped. "Really? Where do you *live*?"

"Finch and – actually, Bloor West Village now." Rae shrugged. "I just moved, I keep forgetting." They were almost at the door.

"It must be a long bus ride!"

"I don't mind." The sun felt like an object weighing on Rae's neck above her collar. She tasted grit in her mouth. Her skirt was too tight and she was going to have so many new messages when she got back to her desk. "I get time to think."

She flattened her hair behind her ears, watched Andy mirror the gesture. Hamid was whistling, so off-key it took Rae several bars to recognize *Dora Dora Dora the Explorer*. She had learnt it sitting on the floor with Jake glazed over in her arms. She wondered where Hamid had heard it.

Another car grated past, then stopped in front of them. The passenger door opened slightly. Hamid muttered, "Fire lane, people."

It was Rae's car, or at least, her name was on the papers. She raised her index finger and didn't look at Hamid, then walked over, a little fast. She pulled the door wider and braced a hand on the roof. "What's wrong?"

She heard Andy whisper loudly, "Who's that?"

Theo squinted at Rae, or at the sun behind her. "Jake got strung by a bee."

"A bee? But . . . the principal's got the kit, those Benadryl tabs? Isn't he at school? It's Tuesday." She looked at her watch, which did not feature the date. "It's Tuesday."

"I *know* it's Tuesday. Can you come?"

She turned. Andy was staring at her own pretty shoes, Hamid at a license plate that read COOLIO. Despite her high collar, the tight waist of her skirt, Rae felt naked.

"Hamid."

He jolted like she'd woken him. "Uh. Huh?"

"I have to go. Can you – "

"Go? Go where?"

Andy: "Is something wrong?"

Rae straightened away from the car. Theo was probably rolling his eyes at the sunvisor. She said, "Hamid, take Andy to the supply closet and get her some hanging folders, and then she can sort all Amelia's old image files. They're on my desk."

"Amelia? She's on disability until October – "

"She's not coming back, Hamid, face it. She is dying and Andy will have to finish her projects. You guys have a nice day. I'll see you tomorrow."

She swung into the car and yanked the door shut.

They were already moving. In the back seat, Marley was sucking the drapery nozzle from the vacuum cleaner.

Theo: "The meds ex*pired,* apparently. I have to bring new ones. We have to."

"Expired? Benadryl expires? This doesn't sound familiar. Did you get a notice?"

"Hell, I don't know, probably. You know what his backpack is like."

Once they were on the road, Rae yanked up her blouse and undid the top button of her skirt before kneeling backwards to lean over and touch Marley's warm sticky face.

"Hel-*lo*, ass."

"Funny." She flushed, canted her hips away from him, stroked Marley's sweaty curls. The skirt really was way too tight. "They have no other Benadryl, from some other kid's kit? It's not like it's prescription."

"Said they couldn't administer drugs other than parent-supplied. So they've been waiting."

"Where were you?"

"Bah blah black blax blah!" Marley babbled happily.

"I had to get her dressed, and that guy who came to fix the stove wouldn't leave, and you don't seem to pick up *your* phone a hell of a lot."

"Shit." She hooked her belly harder into the seatback.

"Yeah, and – Could you sit down, please?"

"I hope *your* Benadryl hasn't expired." Rae sat and looked at Theo. His hair was as bright blond as Marley's. His left hand with no wedding ring was on the wheel. The thin wire arm of his glasses was rucked up above his ear, he hadn't shaved, he was wearing an Eels tee with the first E starting to peel. It was strange to see him mid-week.

"It had. The drugstore also played a role in the past little while."

"Poor kid, all covered in hives. I hope they remember that he's not the one with the *fatal* allergy. It think that's the Yee girl. Jake'd lose it if they took him to the ER."

"Mrs. Dreven isn't a moron. But he'll freak regardless. I thought he'd want you."

"Thanks." Theo had a bit of a tan. He hadn't last weekend when he picked up the kids. Perhaps he'd taken them to the park, or mowed the lawn. She missed the lawn, dark and uneven, mainly moss under the apple tree. "I'm sorry about the phone."

"Could you just look in the bag and see if you recognize the one with the right dosage?" Theo was waving his naked hand around. "They musta – I dunno, changed the colour of the box or something? So I brought them all."

"What, really? Those things cost a fortune. You – "

"This is not the best day I ever had, Rae."

Rae was aware of her breath and his slowly synching up. "Where's the bag?"

"Behind you."

She twisted again to kneel half on the glovebox, her wide office-work ass in the windshield, her hip brushing Theo's shoulder. She had to lean to reach the bag. Marley's yellow sneaker kicked her hard in the jaw.

"So, how's work?"

"Awful." Rae flumphed back into her seat. "Bloody cheese-eaters."

Theo was speeding, passing on the right. "What's new?"

"They've hired this girl, new designer." Rae dumped the boxes on her knees, flicking them over to find instructions. "She's straight out of school, jittery as a jailbreak, knows nothing. They're going to eat her like a scone."

"A *scone*? Pretty?"

"Pretty enough, cream scone. You saw her, back there." Rae plucked a box out of the pile. "This one isn't even Benadryl, it's something else. We can't give him that."

"Eh-he-he-heeee . . . ." Marley was starting to fuss.

"Shush, baby almost there. Yeah, *very* pretty, but – "

"*Very?* The point is, training her will set me back a month."

"But a *scone*?"

"And it'll be me who does. Ursula abdicates all responsibilities except for yelling, Hamid's got something *wrong* with him whenever there's a female around. Amelia is gone and . . ." A pillbox slid between her knees, then another. She grabbed one and waved it. "Theo, I don't recognize *any* of these. I don't think you got the right one."

"What?" He flicked his hands off the wheel in a helpless, ringless gesture, and then grabbed it again when the car skewed. "We're almost there."

She didn't know what he would do with his ring, if he would keep it on his body somewhere, like her, or if it was just lying on the dusty bureau. She missed the bureau. "I thought it was purple. I don't remember. We can't just give him a random pill."

"Look, listen." Theo was flushed under his tan. Marley was a steady drone of disquiet. "His school file has the instruction form, what dosage they're supposed to *administer*. We'll ask to read that. They'll think we're bad parents but they'll let us."

"Oh, ok, yeah. Poor Jake. We *are* bad parents." The baby started sobbing loudly, hands balled into fists. Rae twisted again, boxes sliding onto the floor. "Marley, baby, sh-shh. Oh, hey, you dropped your . . . drapes attachment."

As she brushed her face past Theo's, he said, "Hey, are you crying?"

"Of course she's crying, have you lost your hearing?"

"*You*. Rae. Are *you* crying?"

Saliva had gummed lint and a Cheerio onto the nozzle. Rae wiped the grey plastic carefully on the silk of her left breast before letting Marley's pearl fingers seize it.

Rae sat yet again and reached over her knees to begin gathering the boxes. "No, I'm just – " Her voice shook; tears dripped onto the children's antihistamines. "Oh." She put her wet cheek on her knee and stopped moving.

She could hear the swish of cars whirring past, the suck of Marley's mouth on plastic, the faint brush of denim against napped upholstery as Theo shifted in his seat. He put his palm on her back, across the band of her bra. It was humiliating, knowing he could feel the sobs that filled her lungs, the ridge of fat pushed up by the elastic, but she couldn't stop.

She felt the weight of his hand all through the cloverleaf curve, three stoplights, the bump-bump into the elementary school lot. Theo was driving badly, one-handed. He pulled the parking brake, Theo always did, and took the keys out of the ignition.

His voice, soft: "Just stay with the babe a second, I'll go in."

She raised her head to look at his crooked glasses, his squint-eyed sorrow. "Couldn't we just . . . all go together?"

To: All onsite employees; all temporary employees
CC: Purchasing; Sanjeet Rafeal
From: Reception
Re: Supply Cupboards

Thursday, 8:11 a.m.

Dear Dream Team,

Please note that small items of stationery supplies are available for your use in the supply cupboard of **your department.** If the item that you need is not available in that cupboard, it is **your** responsibility to ask the person in your department responsible for the monthly order (usually the departmental assistant, but not always) to include your item in the next order by submitting a **supplies requisition** (you can find this form on the Dream.Net site). It is **NOT ACCEPTABLE** to remove items from the cupboards of other departments, where supply needs and ordering schedules may be different.

Plan ahead to avoid inconveniencing yourself and your colleagues.

Best,
Reception

HOW TO KEEP
YOUR DAY JOB

DO A DRY RUN ON THE BUS the week before you start, at the right time of day, carrying the right amount of stuff, in the stiff uncomfortable black shoes you can't run in. If you don't own such shoes, buy some. Don't get paint on them.

Also, buy a second alarm clock. Set it half an hour early. Promise your boyfriend that you'll turn it off as soon as it rings, and that you'll get ready really quietly. In the dark if you have to.

You can wear most reasonable clothing to an office; it isn't as bad as all that. Just nothing with paint or an amusing slogan on it, and nothing that makes you look either really attractive or really awful. Probably nothing purple, either. If in doubt, put a cardigan over it.

Smile as you turn off the alarm. Smile on the bus. Smile in the lobby. Smile at your desk.

Put your full name on all paperwork, even though your boyfriend makes fun of your middle name. Accept whatever desk you are given, even if it is in a hallway and someone seems to be asking if that is ok with you. Laugh at whatever jokes you are told, even if they seem sort of mean to gay people.

Work hard.

Don't work so hard that you don't take a lunch. The first day, bring something interesting to eat, although certainly nothing with a weird smell, or even any smell at all if you can help it. Then wait and see if people invite you to eat with them. Interesting food will give people something to talk to you about if they invite you to eat with them. If they don't, eat your complicated odourless sandwich alone at your desk at 2:30.

Smile in the hallways, even when people don't smile back. Smile at the photocopier, even when it's jammed and smears toner on your cardigan when you try to unjam it. Never smile in the washroom.

Don't do anything that could draw attention. Your goal should be to be anonymously indispensable (like a photocopier that never jams). Examples of attention-drawing activities include: putting up posters for your art show, getting loudly angry at your boyfriend on the phone, falling down the stairs, or crying when someone yells at you.

Use Post-its, all the different colours. Use a mechanical pencil. Use Excel spreadsheets, Internet radio, GoogleEarth, and a speakerphone. Use XpressPost and bicycle couriers and the colour scanner and too many paper clips. Revel in all that is yours to use, though you don't need or want to.

When you talk about your boyfriend, start saying *partner,* even though you know he would give you a dirty look if he could hear. In an office, everyone is assumed PC and judgey until proven otherwise.

If ever you arrive late, don't say a thing, least of all an excuse. Act like you thought the workday really started at 9:47. But don't eat lunch, as penance.

Do not moan to your partner that you are imprisoned away from your real life, squashed and stifled, unmotivated and underappreciated. He'll only tell you to move the canvases out of the living room if you're not going to work on them. Your partner hates whiners.

Watch your step.

Watch the movie *American Pie,* particularly that girl from *Buffy* with the "This one time at band camp . . ." refrain. Avoid becoming the loser who is cool somewhere else, not here, and wants people to believe it. You can talk about your surreal still-lifes and your partner's band, but keep in mind: most people don't care. And how cool are you even elsewhere, really?

Even in summer, don't stress about tattoos. Everybody has one now; a butterfly on your shoulder isn't even interesting anymore. If in doubt, put a cardigan over it.

If, because relationships are stressful and his band has been fighting and the summer's been hot, your partner knocks you into the wall and it leaves a bruise, a cardigan will cover that too. You might be able to call the Employee Assistance Program to talk it over, but they probably report everything to management. Nobody likes a whiner.

Do not complain to your colleagues that you are imprisoned away from your art, that your partner is cold and distant, that the photocopier is broken. Your co-workers have problems, too, and will not feel sorry for you. And – remember – nobody likes a whiner.

Your colleagues might not like you even if you don't whine, but you have to pretend they still might. If someone says your clothes are "interesting" because they are "apparently" reversible or that they "can't help but notice" that you are "able to resist" hairstyling products, give them the benefit of the doubt.

If your yoghurt disappears from the fridge, give everyone the benefit of the doubt.

If, at 4:07, a superior finds something that must be completed by the next morning, say you can't stay if you can't stay. Explain that to do overtime, you'll need some notice because you have lots of responsibilities (use the words *overtime* and *responsibilities* – they are more imposing than *work late* and *stuff to do*). If your superior doesn't respond, explain about the show, the workshop, or your partner's desire to have you home by six. Then look sad. Then go sit down and do the work.

Breathe.

If your partner tells you he needs the space to stay out all night, try to understand, but also explain that you feel lonely and worried when he does this. Then try to be sexier. Then look sad. Then go to bed alone.

If people ask you for things that aren't part of your job, try anyway. If you can't do those things, find out whose job it is and tell him or her to do it. If he or she implies that you are lazy, assure them you are not. If they disagree, go sit down and do their work.

Despite your best efforts, you still might fall down the stairs. That's natural. We are all hurtling through space at alarming speeds and those stiff shiny shoes are treadless and not designed for grip. And life is complicated enough that stairs might not be the first thing on your mind.

Accept the possibility of the fall. To be prey to gravity is to be human. But if falling, do stop when you can. *Don't* be seduced by the free fall, the absence of responsibility from the complications of life, the new angles at which a broken leg can bend. Weigh your body hard on each step until you come to one on which you can rest.

Rest.

It's ok.

Check if you are breathing. You might have stopped, for the pain or the shock of the drop.

Breathe.

Check for breakages: limbs, spine, heart.

Are you breathing? Are you broken?

It's ok. Whatever the answer, it is ok.

Breathe.

Open your eyes, even though stairwells are unattractive places, and illuminating windows are unlikely. Regard the grey or beige or greyish-beige walls. Concentrate on their solidity, immobility, inability to do you any harm . . . or help.

Help, or something like it, will come. Heavy footsteps on the landing above you indicate a man with some sense of his own authority. Whoever it is, it's probably no one whose presence can comfort you. You will want your partner, but remember: he doesn't want you, and just signed the lease on a bachelor apartment. You'll want to sob like a rock star, or scream like a soccer-mom, or curse like a CEO, but don't.

Wait. Wait and see what happens next.

Don't throw the baby out with the bathwater.

Don't cut off your nose to spite your face.

Don't get too big for your britches.

Don't quit your day job.

Wait on your stair, whatever stair you've managed to stop at. Lie still.

No matter who is up at the top of the stairs, don't bother to try to look business-casual, to stop crying and straighten your clothes, tuck your hair behind your ears, to stop being hurt or heartbroken or human. Don't even wipe your face – you'll just smear snot, tears and blood across your nice clean cardigan. Blood stains everything, you know.

What is going to happen happens, and that's "Hey, you ok?"

Don't let the colloquial diction fool you. This query is not light. He can see blood on your shin, on the side of you mouth from the fall, and the bruise on your collarbone from last weekend. Even the old bruise hurts now. Your calm, even breathing does not obscure the pain. You aren't fooling anyone, you know.

He will probably touch you, on the shoulder or arm perhaps, because the bubble of business-casual propriety has already been breached by injury, tears, snot. And instead of irritated or sexually harassed, you will feel very slightly comforted by this stranger's touch, and then profoundly ashamed of that.

Think about your ergonomic chair upstairs, the strength in your spine.

He'll say something strikingly banal, like, "Fell?"

Something will clog the back of your throat: maybe blood, or vomit, mucus, dignity. You open your lips and nothing pours out, which is something. But no words, either, just the silence of your bloodied lip, a tooth-bitten cut, not internal hemorrhaging. Remember that you've made your own damage.

The man's tie dangles into your eyeline, and then he lowers onto your stair. He puts his hand back on your shoulder, and says, "Well, don't fret, I'm on the health and safety committee – I know what to do. We gotta assess the damage." He reaches into his jacket pocket.

Your leg is probably broken, just above the ankle, where the bone is close to the surface. Something there is digging and jagged, you feel it without looking down.

Don't look down.

Fine, if it will make you feel better: adjust your cardigan to cover the bruise, but remember that this man doesn't care.

What he pulls from his pocket is not a splint, bandages, sedatives or liquor. It's a cellphone, just like yours, the one that comes free with the two-year contract.

If you are still woozy from the drop, it might help to focus on something solid and singular. Focus on this man's flushed face, his stubble under the silver cellphone as he presses it to his big flat ear. His voice bounces loud off the hard stairwell walls, "Hey, Steve-o. Gregster here. We've got a faller on the southwest stairs, below three, damage to the . . . the fe . . ."

You know he wants to say *femur*, because that's the famous interesting bone on television medical dramas. But that's the thigh bone. That's not the one you broke.

Watch him think and think. He doesn't *know* what bone you broke. But he comes up with something; he is a man doing his job and he does it ok. "Damage to the shin bone, plus pretty shaken up. Call it in, wouldja? I'll get'er down. Bring a car . . . yep. Ten-four. Roger. Ok. Bye now." He does it smooth and fast enough, you have to give credit there.

He meets your gaze. He has swimming-pool coloured eyes. He says, "We have to document this," and you think, suddenly, of all the documents on your desk, things undone. A certain number will never be needed, true, but certain mailings are important, pressing, will be noticed if undone.

You have a headache that could be a concussion. Your lip is bleeding onto your cardigan. You think your right top incisor is loose. And your leg is broken. You feel dangerously close to whining.

There's an invoice that needs to be sent out. You should do it. You probably could do it, if you could lean on this gentleman beside you, or someone. You've been trying to get ahold of your ex-partner all week to give him back the guitar picks and combs and Kerouac of his that you've found. But you think he's screening, or he's changed his cell number.

Don't be too concerned about what's been left behind.

The phone is still open, silver bright. The man isn't speaking on it anymore. He speaks to you instead. He says, "Hike up your hem, please." Staring into the depths of his chlorinated eyes, you wonder what he means, until he looks down at your strange-angled ankle, and you understand what you have to do.

You have to.

If you think to say, *Tibia*, don't, he'll find out. If you think to ask him how many sick days you are entitled to, don't, you'll find out. If you've been thinking about calling your ex's mother, his bandmates, that supermarket checker he sort of likes, and telling them all of his crimes, don't – they'll find out.

Be a class act. Be the bigger person. Be a model employee.

Pull the cuff of your Gap on-sale dress pants gently, smoothly, away from the jut of bone. Don't worry about making the folds even. Don't worry about what this man, Gregster, is thinking, or seeing, or judging. You are colleagues collaborating on a project, the project of accident documentation.

He is saying, "We just gotta record this, you know, for the accident report." It seems that this is not a written report, though, since he doesn't ask you a single question – not your name or your pain threshold or why you find yourself in this strange lame building. Not even whether you are single, if there isn't someone who loves you that should be called on the health & safety cellphone. He won't require a word from you, just flick the phone until it's a camera. He doesn't care, and neither should you.

Then, before you fully realize the state of your blood-painted face, your rucked-up clothes, akimbo angle of your leg and the edge of collar where that bruise might show, he will have taken your picture. Frozen forever, bleeding in the stairwell, in your cardigan.

Don't cry.

Don't even hate him. What else could he do? For you, a stranger with eyeliner running down onto your clavicle, breath all hiccupy, tears tangling your hair, his best emotion is probably only pity. For you in a similar nest of misery last week, your ex couldn't even manage that; only rage that you aren't what he wants, though he thought you were.

Let it go, all of it. You don't really have a choice, anyway. The Gregster is already sliding his palm around your shoulders.

When he says, "Allyoop," push up on your unbroken leg, but let him take as much of your weight as he will. Let your body press into him to keep from falling. It's ok; this isn't sexual, though it's hardly professional. Though he might be blushing as you try to balance, you have no cause to be embarrassed; his job is to help you in this your hour, or week or month, of need.

Don't cry.

Just walk down the stairs.

Don't think about the severity of the breakage, the horror of crutches on public transit, improper stairwell maintenance, or invoice day on Thursday. Don't think about the drawers in your dresser that are empty because he took all his socks and underwear, but don't think about the time he called you a waste of space in front of your brother, either.

The short-term disability, drug-plan reimbursement, gift baskets will all come through to you, just like the forms you filled out so carefully back at the beginning promised. You will wind up with six-weeks of full pay before you must return to your over-due-invoice encrusted desk. As the fragments of your tibia slowly knit back into place, so will a lot of things, or at least begin to. In the meantime you have only to hop down the stairs, straighten your blouse, cry if you must but delicately and without snot. Be the person Steve-o expects to see when he brings the car around.

Breathe.

Keep going forward.

You have a job to do.

SWEET

SYL HAD PUT UP PICTURES of Brian in every room in the house – she had the ones Evan and Angie emailed printed at Black's because she wanted the baby around all the time, as if he lived in their house instead of so far away. The snapshot in the kitchen was from the boy's first moments on earth, flushed and scrunched, pink and blue, wailing and naked. Even Laurence could admit he smiled at the little striver whenever he opened the fridge.

Under the gaze of the magneted picture, Syl had been cooking all day. Margarine tubs of stew, lasagna, and taco casserole, labeled in ballpoint on masking tape, were bricked in the freezer, fortifications against her husband's ruin.

When Laurence finally, slowly came downstairs from the office, Syl was at the counter, chopping vegetables. The room smelled of unseen fruit and sugar. "Get everything done?" She began plopping celery sticks into an orange Tupperware half-full of water.

He sat awkwardly at the kitchen table: left hip canted up, weight on the cane, watching her. "Mainly. Muellers' dog barked for a while. Got a couple emails to write up tonight."

"I hate that damn dog. Those boys take advantage of you; you retired so you wouldn't have to write emails in the evenings."

Laurence grunted.

Syl sighed. "So there's celery in the orange and carrots in the blue one, and I'll do just one salad because that will wilt after the second day . . . ."

"The travel agent got back to you?"

"It's booked." She hacked sharply through the flared part of a celery stalk. "Direct to Seoul. The lady said I got a good deal for $1,200."

Laurence whistled. "If you say so. I still don't see – "

"It's not like we can't afford it." Syl waved her hand, seemingly dismissing the whole abundant house, thick drapes and satellite radio and all. "Angie called me in tears, Laurence, and Evan could barely form a sentence, he was so tired. Brian cried nearly the whole night. Again. At least I can sit up with him."

"Evan and Angie are almost 30. They'll survive."

"Well, of *course*. But we could help them do a little better than that."

Laurence watched her snap the lid onto the orange container. "*We?*"

"There's still room on the flight . . . ?"

He pictured his webmail homepage, all those bold-faced unread messages, the nuclear-bright streets of Korea.

"I'm still healing." He gestured down at the knob of swell and bandages bulging through the knee of his trousers. "And the boys at the office, you know . . ."

"It's *been* healing a while now. And Ev is your *own* boy."

"Sanjeet and Mark *ask* for my help. Ev, thus far, has not."

The oven timer dinged, turning her towards it.

"You're really going to go, just cross the world? Do you even know about the lunatic in the north and his missiles? How are you going to get to Evan's place? You can't just expect everyone to understand English." He imagined Seoul ominous and vague, narrow streets, shouted strangeness, labyrinthine confusion.

She gripped the oven door. Blue veins showed in her thin white skin, but it was still smooth. She was three years younger than Laurence; if she'd worked, she wouldn't have been retired yet. "Ev will meet me at the airport." She opened the oven, bent her round bottom towards him. "Well, at least the pie turned out."

112

"You know I've never cared for sweets." For some reason, this had always been a lie he enjoyed telling. "And if I needed something, I'm sure I could make it myself." That one was new.

"Well." Syl straightened with the pie and hipped the oven shut, hard. "This one cherry pie is for Mr. Carbone. Not sweets, just sweet."

"Corey Carbone?"

"You can take it over tomorrow. I saw him go out this morning, and with the Muellers' cats around, I hate to leave it on the step."

Laurence leaned back in the chair and a gentle pain swabbed at his knee. "Those cats are a menace – should be able to leave a pie for a few hours without fear. I'm gonna plant some marigolds next year."

"It's bugs that hate marigolds. You'll take the pie to Mr. Carbone?"

"Fine. But what do cats hate, then?"

"You, I'd imagine. We have to leave in three hours."

*

The afternoon was cool and bright, deep sunny fall. He couldn't drive her with the knee still weak, but he went along in the taxi, through baggage check and all the way to customs. When they came to the "Passengers with boarding passes only" sign, Syl had a crisis of conscience. Laurence sighed and fiddled with her carry-on. Always when things were paid for, she regretted.

"You *know* you can't put the margarine tubs in the microwave, right? You have to dump them out on a plate, and then drape a paper towel over so it doesn't splatter."

"I *live* in the *house*, Sylvia. I know how things work."

"Are you *sure* you'll manage? I mean – " she held up a hand " – with your knee and all."

He was bent over, one hand raised above his head to grip the cane, the other tugging her bag's zipper tight. He gazed up innocently. "And if I wouldn't?"

She relaxed at this, rolled her eyes. Then he straightened and hugged her with his hands tight at her shoulder blades. When she walked away down the long blue-carpeted hallway, he felt as if the plane had crashed into the sea.

*

The evening was much the same as any. He showered and checked his email in his bathrobe (his brother updating his birding life list; lawyer-joke forward from former colleague; thanks from the young turks at the office for projections he'd sent). Then he watched *The National* while sitting on the foot of the bed, until there was a story about Kim Jong Il's plutonium stores. Laurence shivered, and flipped off the set before the human-interest story about llamas, which weren't human anyway, and slept quietly on his side of the bed. He dreamt of kimchi, a food he had never eaten but was surely vile.

It was the next morning that things really started to go to hell.

He did seven crossword clues waiting for toast before recalling that Syl kept the toaster unplugged for fear of electrical fires. Straight from the fridge, the butter was hard and punctured the bread. He forgot to make the tea until he wanted to drink it, and then the first bag he found turned out to be utterly not Earl Grey but something gingery that promised, upon inspection of the packet, to ease gas pains *with natural effectiveness*. He didn't know what that meant or what this product was doing in his home.

Laurence slopped tea down the sink and was half-way to the door and a steeped Tim Hortons' tea before he recalled he'd had his right knee replaced six weeks ago and couldn't press the gas or brake. He was, as usual, devastated.

After the newly found and brewed Earl Grey (in the back of the cupboard, behind the celery salt – why?) and torn-up cold toast, the day clenched before him, thick and dense as rainforest. He did ten across – "megaton" – read a few lines of a movie review – "compelling fluff." Finally Laurence hauled himself up, nodded at enraged and distant Brian (in actual fact, he spoke to the baby, as he often did when alone. This time it was, "Why you gotta cause us all such heartache, huh?") and went to the kitchen window.

On both sides of the street, neighbours were departing on their days of useful employment. He could only see a few driveways through the oak leaves, but with the dual-income trend, he got to witness seven individuals striding down their driveways with purpose, energy, briefcases.

Then it was 9:30, on a weekday morning in Indian summer. His inbox had no new messages and he couldn't walk even as far as Tim Hortons and everyone he loved was in Korea, where it was the middle of the night. Laurence Brunswick was a 66-year-old man with all of his mental faculties, and most of his physical ones, who was only four crossword clues away from utter redundancy.

Corey Carbone lived four houses down from the Brunswicks. He was in his eighties, though Laurence couldn't fathom who in the 1920s would have named a boy-child *Corey*. The Carbone mailbox, with an orange cardinal painted on it, seemed to have always been a fixture of the street, but in decades of four-houses-downness, the two men had only exchanged half-waves over car roofs and muttered apologies over windblown recycle bins. Syl took the neighbours all their misdirected mail, did all the chatting about tulip bulbs, all the neighbourly surveillance from the veranda. She had always been more than equal to all the block parties and yard sales and, until retirement, Laurence's work had been so richly complex and demanding that his own four walls were as much beyond it as he could handle.

One summer morning about eight years prior, Syl had been watering the Freesia when she realized that Corey Carbone had not come out to check his hummingbird feeder by 11:30, an event that traditionally marked the end point in her gardening mornings. Syl had noted over the past several years that the gentleman four houses down had become, if not infirm, then perhaps "less active." But he always minded the bird feeders – hummingbird syrup in summer, finch seeds in winter – once before noon and once after. Until the day that he didn't.

Syl had sat on a lawn chair with a glass of lemonade (Laurence was imagining now; he didn't know this part of the story) waiting for Corey Carbone to emerge. And he hadn't and he hadn't and that afternoon Sylvia Brunswick chopped extra apples and kneaded extra pastry and baked an extra pie for Corey Carbone. And extended her lunch break long enough to bring it over to him, and discovered him lying behind the azaleas, having suffered a stroke on the way to the bird feeder. His clothes were covered with sticky red syrup.

Laurence came to know of this only because that night at dinner, their own pie seemed less full of apples than usual. Syl replied that the doubled recipe had not quite worked out, and that she had spent three hours in the emergency room with the man four houses down because he'd had a medium-severity stroke. This, in addition to causing Laurence to doubt his wife's arithmetic skills, had given him some confusion. The other pie, it turned out, had been left at the nurses' station.

Laurence accepted a tiny piece of pie, to calm her. He could not imagine his wife at the bedside of a stranger – would she be teary, or as firmly practical as she was on family vacations? He pictured the same sort of chaos, uncertainty, with gurneys instead of roller coasters.

When Laurence had been wheeled down the hall with a cartilage knee and returned with a plastic one, he learned how Syl behaved in a hospital – just as he'd suspected, as she did at Disneyworld – but he still could not picture her with this stranger, Corey Carbone. But this was not a comment on Corey

Carbone; Laurence had difficulty seeing Syl anywhere he himself was not present.

Now, Laurence was accountable to this stranger for one pie. He peered into the fridge at slightly fogged saran over the pink-and-white lattice. Syl's handiwork was solid and elegant, both saran and pastry. The kitchen still smelled of ginger. At Disneyworld she clutched the purple-shaded map and grinned at Evan's excitement and refused to go on any of the rides herself. He missed her.

He shut the fridge and did a limping lap of the house, observing the dead hang of curtains, mounds of molted shoes in the bottoms of closets. Syl's white handbag, the summer one, was on top of the hamper in the guest bathroom, like hidden treasure. He sat down on the toilet lid to open it, but it was only full of bobby pins.

One more lap and back to the kitchen window to gaze at Syl's dead fall flower bed, of all the years past, until he was good and depressed. Back at the fridge, Brian silently shrieked at the injustice of his exile from his homeland, his people, his grandfather. Laurence balanced the pie on his free palm, and, leaning heavily on his cane, shuffled to the door.

*

Corey Carbone's lawn was smooth as a tucked-in bedsheet, but the flower beds were all woodchipped over, the bird feeder empty, and the cement of the third stairs had cracked. By the time Laurence reached the porch, Corey Carbone was standing behind his screen door, leaning leftwards on something out of view, watching him.

"Hello, Brunswick." Corey Carbone was short, jowly and bald; it was hard to make out finer details through the screen. The hem of his fawn-coloured bowling shirt hung several inches in front of his fly, suspended by a stiff spherical gut. His voice was nervous, high-pitched, and slightly slurred; like a drunk waiting to get hit. "What brings you by?"

"Well, I don't mean to bother you, Mr. Carbone."

"Oh, oh, no." He still did not open the door.

"You know how Syl loves to bake." Laurence gestured with the pie, but the head beyond the screen remained impassive. Suddenly furious for Syl's wasted effort, his own wasted painful walk, Laurence bent awkwardly to set the pie on a Muskoka chair. "She baked you this pie, asked me to drop it off. The pie is from Syl. Hope you enjoy."

"Thank you," said Corey Carbone, voice even squeakier than before.

Laurence nodded sharply, pivoted on the cane-tip, and called, "You're welcome. It's cherry," as he staggered down the steps. For all he knew, Corey Carbone watched him stump all the way to the sidewalk. So what if he did?

*

Once the pie was gone, that and his family became all that Laurence craved. He regretted letting Syl's beautiful pastry go to that ingrate with the silly name, and he regretted Brian's unseen colic across the ocean, and his son and daughter-in-law's stress and distress. He regretted the boys at the office, Mark and Sanjeet, their nervous idiocy driving the company closer and closer to ordinary. He supposed his own life had been ordinary, in some ways. Many ways. It hadn't seemed so at the time.

He thought about all the cakes and pies Syl had baked for Evan. There was so much less after the boy moved out, because of Laurence's insistence on not liking sweets. Now he pictured sloppy swirls of blue icing on a birthday cupcake, imagined the cool grit of coconut cream. He remembered Evan sticky and greedy, reaching for more while Laurence nibbled unnoticed on a "sliver."

To Brian's snapshot, he revealed his years of sugar dishonesty. "Chocolate-chip cake, gingersnaps, black-bottom pie, peach coffee cake ... they're all sublime, when she makes them. Every birthday, she made herself a lemon pie, shaved little bits of the rind onto the meringue." The microwave pinged, interrupting Laurence's chat with the fridge door and embarrassing him somehow. He silently took his reheated lasagna to the table. Throughout the meal, Laurence mourned the pie he could not eat for dessert. There was nothing suitably sweet in the pantry, not even boxed cookies or a tin of pears – he'd already checked.

When Syl called – he had just closed his still-empty inbox – he was spellbound at his desk for forty-five minutes, listening to her tales of flight delays, kimchi, baby wipes. He could hear Brian rioting in the background, a fierce soprano siren. She described this fat angry grandson, then her emaciated son and his 80-hour workweeks, exhausted Angie's obsession with Dr. Spock.

Despite knowing the per-minute costs, Laurence asked about the city, the luggage, her health (but not the ginger tea), their meals. Then he asked, casually, chattily, almost academically, about pie. It was only when she said the baby was spitting up that Laurence consented to let her go.

The next morning, he dug through the basement deep freeze, frost beading his cheeks, until he found the cottage-cheese container marked "Pie cherr. 09" in Syl's tight cursive. The pastry recipe on the back of the lard box took most of the morning, but it finally cohered into something resembling a pie shell. It was early afternoon before Laurence finally put the fruit into a saucepan. After twenty minutes of ardent stirring, medium heat, and a half-pound of sugar, the cherries showed no evidence of a will to be pie. There was a tap at the back door.

Once again, Laurence saw Corey Carbone's big baby face through a screen door. This time, though, his arm was draped around a small Filipina woman.

It was Laurence's turn to say, "Yeesss?"

The woman beamed blankly until Corey Carbone said, "Came to thank you. For the pie."

"It was from Syl." Laurence waved his wooden spoon absently.

The woman took this as invitation to open the door wide and gracefully pilot the big man through. She looked like a nymph dancing with a tree. Laurence let his irritation go as soon as he saw the sweat glistening on the side of Corey Carbone's neck.

Laurence set the spoon in the spoon rest, and padded (still barefoot at two p.m., with company!) over to the woman who was manipulating Corey Carbone into the kitchen chair closest to the stove. It was not Laurence's dinner seat, but it was the one he sat in when Syl was cooking and he was watching her. His guest looked so thankful to finally be safely seated that Laurence could not begrudge him the spot. The woman began backing away.

"I come later?"

"Yes, Ciara, thanks." Corey Carbone leaned back cautiously. Without the screen door intervening, Laurence could see that Corey Carbone's face was smooth-shaven, with the right side mannequin-still. If there were such things as old-man mannequins.

"When I come back? How long?"

"I won't stay long, Brunswick."

Laurence breathed in deeply through his nose. "I'll take you home, Mr. Carbone. No need to trouble . . . her." He had forgotten the name already. Pathetic.

When the woman was gone, Corey Carbone shrugged and smiled, and his tiny voice said, "Sorry about this. She tries to get me out of the house regular. But she don't think too much about where besides *out*. Sorry."

Laurence smiled – the second apology was all he needed to feel generous. "No trouble at all. Syl's more the stickler for scheduling than I am." Another lie from the clear blue. Laurence felt like cupping it fondly in his palm.

"Whatcha making? Another pie?"

Laurence considered. Finally: "Bake sale. Church. Syl wouldn't want them to miss the donation, just because she had to go out of town." He was staring into the pot of bubbling watery cherries. It looked liquid, drinkable, utterly un-pie-like.

A shift of chair legs. "Things all *right*, Brunswick? Syl's ok?"

He saw an expectation of tragedy in Corey Carbone's leftside features – not smug, only fearful. "A celebration, actually. Our first granbaby got born. How 'bout that?" Where had the slang come from? To match Corey Carbone's happy-hour slur, perhaps.

"How 'bout *that*? *Fan*tastic, Brunswick." Corey Carbone slapped his right knee and Laurence winced. "Boy or girl?"

"Boy. Brian. Seven weeks." Laurence pointed at the fridge picture – the fat mottled face and blue-veined skull. All children were ugly at birth, but Brian looked like a champion anyway. The cherries were making little splashing noises. "Syl's gone to help out a bit." When Laurence bent over the pot, red bubbles popped and splattered his arm.

"Glad for the quiet? Or you miss 'er?"

Laurence turned down the burner, frowning.

"I could never stand it, myself. Rysa and I spent maybe ten nights apart, all told. Maybe less."

"Rysa?" Laurence searched his mind for an image of a woman in the Carbone driveway, but he came up empty. It was another strange name, or perhaps only a standard one that Corey Carbone's tongue could no longer render. He hoped she wouldn't turn out to be a Doberman as he asked, "You folks were married a long time?"

"Thirty-five years, but that don't seem long when you start at eighteen."

Laurence did the math from the apparent age of the man – Corey Carbone had likely been a widower for twenty years. The cherries were starting to sink in the goop. He stirred forlornly. "In all those years of married life, Rysa ever tell you how to make a cherry pie?"

"Well, no, not that I . . . Why?"

"*Why?* What do you – That's what I'm *doing* here. *Trying* to do."

Silence. Laurence looked up. Corey Carbone sat with both legs kicked forwards, one elbow on the chair arm, the other hand rested atop his cane, which was leaning on his thigh. It should have been a casual pose, but for Corey Carbone's stiff body, it looked like the rack. "Sorry, Brunswick." He shrugged; only the left shoulder rose.

Laurence sighed. "Sorry, man, sorry. Tough morning."

"What's gone wrong? Smells good."

Laurence sniffed dismissively. To him, the smell was over-sweet, syrupy, *wrong*. "Thank you. But it's not like a pie filling. From here, it's like cherry soup."

"Such a thing, y'know. Cherry soup. Had it on a cruise once."

"A cruise?" Laurence abandoned the question. "I don't want soup. I want pie. I was trying to boil down the juice to . . . gel, you know. But it won't."

Corey Carbone shook his head, and his jowls wobbled equally on both sides. "Too much juice? Or not enough thickners?"

Laurence stood completely still and felt his neck crack. "Thickener?"

Corey Carbone's good eye squinted. "Whaddya put in?"

"Cherries. Frozen ones." The pebbly pie crust looked greyish in the slight sun through the kitchen window.

"And . . . ?" Corey Carbone nodded stiffly, left-leaning, encouraging.

"Sugar. Because they weren't all that sweet."

"Pie cherries are, uh, sour cherries, yeah. You hafta add the sugar . . . and . . ."

"And . . . ?" Laurence asked. He set the spoon on the spoon-rest. A little of pink dripped on the white stovetop.

"Dunno . . . flour?" Another uneven shrug.

"Flour? Flour goes in the *crust*, I found a recipe for the crust."

"Didja find one for the filling?"

Laurence turned off the stove. "I don't think she uses one. Anyway, I couldn't find it. Her files are a mess." He went over and took a seat at the table.

"First time she's been away in how long?"

"Not that long." Laurence slouched forward, arms on the placemat, chest pressing down. "I used to travel a lot, on business. I only just retired."

"Ah." Corey Carbone grinned. His eyelid and mouth stayed flaccid on the right, but both eyes were bright. "First time *she's* been away in . . . ?"

Laurence whistled. "Ever, I suppose."

"Why didn't *you* go?"

The pink smell of cherries was starting to stifle. Laurence wondered if it would be rude to open a window. "I had work to . . . cover."

"I thought you retired."

"The new team, they need a little saving, sometimes." Laurence had said this dozens of times, always in a hearty, resigned tone. Today, the words sounded almost violent.

Laurence had a momentary flash of Syl's perfect puff of white hair wandering down an ugly alley of thugs and thieves. "Plus, it's hard to travel, laid up like this." He waved his cane, then glanced at Carbone's own and felt bizarrely guilty.

"Oh, well, I'm sure you've seen enough of the world." Corey Carbone squirmed in his chair, both hands pressed on the cane top as he hauled his butt forward, then shifted his weight onto his left hip.

"You all right?"

"S'ok," Corey Carbone said tightly. It was several seconds before he finally leaned back again and relaxed his grip on the cane. "If yer giving up on that pie, we could just eat the cherries, you know. With spoons."

"Pretty sad thing to offer a guest."

"Well, I'll take what I can get. Be a proper dessert with a little ice cream, if you got it."

Laurence got obediently to his feet, though he felt himself listing far more leftward than usual, white-knuckling his own cane. An apology for inhospitality fished around in his brain, but all that came out was, "I think we *might* have, not ice cream but sherbet – " he opened the freezer and foam-white air fogged his glasses " – shoot, sorry, Corey Carbone, it's raspberry." He shut the freezer with a sad thump.

"You think I care about clashing shades of pink?"

"Right." Laurence nodded and reopened the freezer.

"And whatcha call me by my full name for? Think some other Corey will pop in, demand ice cream – sherbet?"

Laurence jolted again. "No, sorry, Carbone. Your name just sorta slides off the tongue all in one piece, you know?"

"Never heard that one. Course, nothing slides off my tongue, these days."

Laurence tried to picture the pre-stroke Corery Carbone, sober-spoken and smooth, or at least not sounding quite so boozily meek. He couldn't. The thin red juice dribbled to the bottom of the bowl, and the cherries clung like slugs to the sherbet. It looked revolting. Laurence took the dishes and spoons to the table, sat and asked, "What was your profession, Carbone? Before you retired?"

Corey Carbone swallowed his first bite and smiled. "Professor. Physics. Quantum. The way I worked, no one does any more. But then, I don't do it either."

The cherries were sickeningly sweet; Laurence figured he'd overdone the sugar in his frustration. Corey Carbone's pants were a shade of an unripe banana, pulled up topside of his gut. He did not look like an intellectual. "You miss it?"

"Must've, once, I guess. Twenty years ago now. Too much else to miss, in the meantime. I miss Rysa, smartest lady in Weston and a damn fine ornithologist. I miss walking to the can without having to hang off that little girl like a lecher." Corey Carbone dug his spoon into his pink mess again. "This is damn good, like that spun sugar crap kids get at the fair." His speech was smoothing out, slightly.

"Cotton candy."

They were silent a moment, eating. Finally, Laurence had to ask, "Corey Carbone, do you remember what happened when you had that stroke, and Syl came over, all that? Could you see her?"

"Sure I remember, sure I saw her, sorta." Corey Carbone smacked his lips, glanced down at his empty bowl, then over at Laurence's, still mainly full. "Sorta long to explain, I guess."

Laurence pushed the pink swirl towards him. "Me, I got nothing but time. You don't mind?"

There was a pink drip of raspberry on Corey Carbone's lower lip that he made no move to lick. It seemed suitable just there, like a beauty mark or a freckle. "You got it right – nothing but time."

To: All onsite employees; all temporary employees
From: Reception
Re: Red Camry, License BKILLA

                          Friday 9:55 a.m.

Your lights are on.

RESEARCH

THE RESEARCH DEPARTMENT at Dream Magazines has been reduced. In straitened economic times, something always has to go, and this time it was knowledge, in the form of four-fifths of the research team. More specifically, these are (were) the suspender-wearing architectural historian whose sexuality could never be determined; the tall willowy former model who ate Altoids by the box; the moonlighting Chinese chef with his mounds of recipes and climbing ivy plant; and the legal expert who received an angry phone call from his ex-wife every day at three p.m.

On Monday morning, they were all already gone by the time the last employed researcher arrived. She was 38 years old and possessed of several credits towards a masters in cultural anthropology; twin teenaged boys; a Nescafé jar on the right corner of her desk; and the lowest salary, least seniority, and least sarcastic sense of humour in the department. Leadership felt they'd settled on a prudent choice.

At first, she did not realize that she had become the sole embodiment of the research department. The baffles of her cube were high enough that she rarely saw her colleagues accidentally, and since they were on flex hours, she often couldn't find anyone even if she tried. So the echoing silence did not bother her when she arrived at 8:55, set her lunch bag (SpongeBob, one of the boys' discarded treasures) in the fridge, prepared her Nescafé in the microwave, and set to work on the last of her research for an article on fastenings in *Dream Beading*.

By 10:06, she had already solved what a grommet was, and had begun the question of what one might do with it. Also at 10:06, the team from Building Services arrived and began to dismantle the cubes of the research room. Because of her hard won ability to tune out the hungover mutterings and heavy footfalls of her (former) colleagues, she looked up only when her own walls came down. A vista of dusty desks and dead plants suddenly opened. Far far at the end of the room was a window she had never noticed before. It beamed pale light over her former colleague's many empty Altoids tins.

Men were walking away with the walls. She knew a corset was laced through a grommet, as was a shoe, and also through a grommet a flag was bound to its pole, but she did not know what was going on. She was alone except for a man with "69" on his T-shirt who was removing the phone that had brought so many calls of marital devastation.

"Where have they gone?" she asked him.

"Who?"

"The rest of the department."

He weighed the phone in his palm. "No one tells me, sorry. I just come to take the phones."

"But . . . but the whole . . . everyone?" She thought for a moment. "Should I be gone too? Did someone forget to fire me?"

"In these straitened economic times, I would not dare to say," said the man with the phone, and then he took it away.

She had never received formal assignments in research – usually her more-senior colleagues just sluffed their least appealing tasks onto her. Without a task, without colleagues, without even walls, Research felt most unmoored. She went, silent in her Payless Maryjanes, to her supervisor's office, though she had been instructed never to go there before noon unless she was dead.

The supervisor's office was empty. More alarming, even the seemingly solid floor-to-ceiling walls that bound it had been removed, so that it was no longer an office at all, merely some space at the end of the hall.

At this point, she had to go research who supervised her supervisor. This turned out to be a junior VP, who was on paternity leave. He was supervised by a senior VP who was at a kitchenware convention. She plunged on through the org chart, only to find that next in the chain of command were the Offices of the CEO.

The men who ran the company, distant from her as Andromeda stars, were no one she could picture asking anything, let alone what came after *grommet*. But if they weren't to provide the next action-item memo, who would? She had never been a self-starter. She was always bolstered by her colleagues. The now-terminated chef had been especially kind, always calling her *kid* and gently punching her shoulder.

He was gone now – they were all gone, but both her boys needed upper *and* lower retainers. She had to steel her soul, stay at her desk, and formulate her own action item. But that was when the 69 guy came back, nodded absently to her, picked up her phone and began to disconnect it.

She slammed her hand down on the keypad. "I'm staying. I'm Research."

"Ah. Sorry." He drew his hand back. "What are you researching?"

"I . . . what do you think I should research?"

He blinked at her, blushed slightly. "I overheard an editor on the fifth floor, someone from *Dream Woman,* say they wanted to run a feature on women's orgasms."

"Seriously?" She was homesick for her old workstation, for when she was secure within walls with a day's docket of concepts to investigate. That morning's *grommet* had been left over from a long, complex assignment, from *hook and eye,* to the *toggle* to the more complex *spring-ring* and *lobster.* Only *grommet* turned out to have nothing to do with the necklaces and bracelets, just a braced hole in fabric. All the others were in the article, but grommet was out, and even that, though sad, was satisfying. How would she know what was in or out if she didn't know what was on the list?

"What, specifically, about orgasms? What questions do they want answered?"

The guy shrugged. "If I were you, I would not limit myself to the simplistic binary of question and answer. Yes, there are many questions worth answering: why is the sky blue? Who are we when we are dead? Is the public fascination with the Gosselins *schadenfreude* or pity? Why do some nations drive on the right and some on the left?"

"Those are the sorts of research items I am used to."

"But there are matters that do not beg a question, only attentiveness. We do not ask questions of a waterfall, of a BMW engine, of a newborn. We must only observe, minutely – through this care we come to know not only the answers but the questions."

She didn't know what to say, but the clock on the wall behind the phone guy's head said 12:30, lunchtime. Actually, it was a sushi clock, so it really said unagi:30, but in any case she was hungry.

Without colleagues for company, Research ate her cheese-and-tomato sandwich while beginning her research on the female orgasm. She read an article about how women are chronically cheated on the pleasures of oral sex. It was surprisingly boring. She took some notes, started the second half of her sandwich, and opened weather.ca. The temperature at Pearson airport was 22 degrees, and skies were clear. That sounded nice. And now that everything and everyone were gone, she needed only to turn to see 22 degrees and clear skies over the airport. The window felt miraculous.

It wasn't miraculous: there were fireworks of bird-shit on the outside and fuzzy grey dust inside. But it was also floor to ceiling, eight feet across: blue light and white contrails and green grass and traffic. It had been a long time since anything had changed in Research, and now everything had changed, even the light.

She stood up and went towards the light until she bonked off the glass: left arm, plastic glasses frame, both breasts. At the airport, a fat-bodied aeroplane lofted up, and a striped windsock whipped. It looked like a lovely day out there but the window frame didn't open, so she had no empirical knowledge of the current weather.

She went to her desk and read about barometric pressures, cool fronts and rising air, and what a windsock means. She didn't glance at the powdery blue sky until the 16:55 commuter rose towards Washington, D.C. It was narrow and glinting in the afternoon sun, like a needle that could thread a grommet. She watched its whole ascent, the perfect stab into the sky, until the tailfins disappeared at the top of the window.

Then her phone rang. She picked it up, held it to her ear and said, "Research."

"This is Ella from *Dream Woman* editorial?" said a hesitant voice. "I was trying to reach my usual research contact, extension 7195? Tall, well-dressed, nice breath?"

"You don't know her name?"

"I knew her extension, but apparently it has changed?"

"She's . . ." Research knew so little. "Gone. She doesn't work here anymore."

"That's awful? I've got this unconventional-orgasm article to fill in . . . ?"

Research missed her pretty, angsty colleague, their chats between stalls in the ladies' room about *Canadian Idol*. But she had a mortgage, a car loan, a taste for out-of-season fruit. "I have some material I could send you."

There was a pause. Perhaps the woman was wondering what sort of person researched unconventional orgasms without being asked. Finally: "Anything good?"

Research completed the call, formatted her notes on vaginal, clitoral, G-spot, and anal, then powered down her computer at 5:03. She took her cardigan from the back of her chair, her lunch sack from under it, and said goodbye to no one. Then she went out to the parking lot. She counted 196 cars as she walked to the bus stop. White was the most common – 68 cars. She could not remember the colours of the four cars now missing.

*

When Research got off the bus at 8:48 the next morning, there was a silver-blue airplane high above her head. It had a fish painted vertically on the tail, as if it was diving. The fish was blue, too, brighter than the plane. Brightest blue of all was the sky.

Indoors was mainly grey but the blue beamed in through the enormous window, which someone somehow had washed, inside and out.

She looked into the exact definition of teal, the blogs of MuchMusic VJs that her sons liked, the calorie content of chili, the average woman's desired amount of oral sex versus experienced. She sent these facts to various editors at *Dream Fashion, Dream Teen, Dream Woman*. She stared out the window. The sky was a medium blue-green, more blue than green: teal.

She walked through vast empty space between her desk and the window – even the other researchers' desks had been removed now. She had always threaded through them like a rope through a grommet, and now there was too much space. She had liked her colleagues; everyone boiled extra water in case someone else wanted tea. She had no way of finding them now, out there in their real lives.

Back at her desk, Research found an enthusiastic email from *Dream Woman* regarding her facts about oral pleasure, requesting further research. The editor did not mention the chili information (surprisingly low fat).

Googling "techniques+cunnilingus" brought many suggestions, but they repeated from website to website, or even within one – "light feathery kisses to the inner thigh" seemed much the same as "light feathery kisses up and down the leg." She wondered how else to research this, eyed the framed photo of her husband in his canoe, and sent off her report.

She boiled a single cup of water for tea. She ate her yoghurt early. She looked out the window at a helicopter rising, possibly carrying the executive team from an internet start-up with a bold innovation for something. She wanted to research using reality, not the Internet. She wanted to be good at her job and interesting to her family. She wanted to slip through life like a lace through a grommet. She wanted to be someone who found joy in more than just what her husband got up to with his tongue.

She stood up. She left her purse in her file drawer and her coat on its hook, but she nevertheless left the research room at a non-standard break time. She didn't know where she was going, but she did know what was available to do at her desk: action items she had created for herself. An encyclopaedia of deposed kings, a list of xylophone-heavy musical scores to be matched to the film, plus a half-dozen more websites she'd been asked to investigate for methods of flicking the tip of the tongue to draw out the shy clitoris. Research could not summon enthusiasm. She found the xylophone shrill and most kings deserving of being deposed, and her own clitoris had never been terribly shy.

She went into the stairwell. She climbed one flight, and was already in an unknown world, though the hallway carpeting was the same platinum grey. Research walked passed a door with a Dilbert cartoon on it, then one with an On Vacation! sign, then a Christmas wreath, then one from which the nameplate had fallen down. She paused by an open door to see someone pulling a computer from the desk. It was the same building services guy that had taken away the phones yesterday, only now his T-shirt read

"Flat-chested." She nodded at him. He blinked, looked around, and then nodded back.

She walked into a kitchen that was the same as the one downstairs but different; like a kitchen in a dream, but unlike anything in *Dream Kitchen* magazine. Here was a toaster oven instead of a pop-up toaster, Dawn detergent instead of No-Name. In the refrigerator, there were glass jars with rubber tops, which Research liked – so easy to investigate. These jars contained chopped cantaloupe and blueberries. No pudding cups, but many yoghurts. Here, salad dressings separated into homemade oil and vinegar rather than emulsified Kraft Italian.

Research wondered if this was a wealthier floor, or simply one that valued lunch products more? She could afford BioBest yoghurt and organic pita, too, and did – for her family, at home. She never thought about the food she ate alone at her desk.

Thoughtfully, she took her pen and pad and began cataloguing this floor's milk/cream ratio, its pears and apples, Snackwiches and Lunchables. Research went on to other fridges on other floors, found breast milk, live-culture yoghurt, crème brûlée. Then the small appliances, and then the walls and ceilings themselves – grape-juice spatters, gum stuck above the wastebin, lipstick kisses on a cupboard door (why?). Lists and descriptions of the kitchen configurations of Dream Inc. took her all the way to the glorious weekend: the boys' basketball practice, a dinner party, a Sunday morning in bed, 69ing with her husband.

On Monday, she began listing contents of above-sink cupboards. She didn't know what else to do. The economy was blowing up and even airplanes sometimes exploded and a sizeable percentage of women never achieved an orgasm. The Internet seemed to promise solutions but she couldn't find them there. Problems like money and pleasure and flight were beyond her to answer alone – she couldn't even form the questions. But she could think of dozens of questions about the people at Dream Inc., and once she started asking, she found she actually cared to know. Even after 5:00, in the grocery store or beside the basket-ball court, she wondered about her colleagues' square inches of monitor size, highway or surface-route commutes, and their confusion over dental plans. She wondered about their happiness, their lunches, their lives. These were trying times, and she was curious about how other people were tried.

In the kitchens, Research encountered very few of the people she was researching. Once beside a sink where she was trying to describe the scent of a label-less bottle of dish soap (pine, lavender, and chlorine?), a lady jostled past to rinse an apple. Once a gentleman in a three-piece suit waited patiently for her to finish counting the pieces in his Corn Bran box (158) and put them all back before he poured out a bowl.

She thought perhaps the rest of the staff was clinging to their desks to avoid detection by the outsourcing committee. Her approach was the opposite, avoiding all the research requests on the pleasures of rimming and stock images of mahogany veneer. She knew if she kept providing those things, someone would notice it was the same over and over, and ask her to stop with three weeks severance. She wanted to offer something new.

As days passed, Research got braver, her questions more intimate in a way that had nothing to do with oral pleasure. She tried inquiries into daily urination volumes (not as much increase relative to proximity to water coolers as she had expected) or favoured workplace plants (climbing ivy, though cloth cubical walls were unclimbable, and most of the ivy wound up straggling over the floor of high productivity cubes or strangling the computer systems of low productivity cubes). She counted one-panel cartoons on bulletin boards (so much *Herman,* after all these years). She felt that this was useful information, or at least interesting. At least, she was interested.

Sometimes she did sit alone in the research room, though she felt like the tallest tree in a lightning storm. She tried to keep up with what the Internet offered, but that seemed to be mainly variations on the direness of the economic downturn (not as bad as the Great Depression . . . or was it?) and that some women liked their vulvas cupped in their partners' palm. Her husband had always been more of a brusher than a cupper, but for the sake of research they tried both in rapid succession, with no significant variation.

This became her life, and her life became ok: counting ivy leaves and learning the CBC3 DJ rotation and sparks-behind-the-eyes orgasms even in the missionary position, contrary to all the best research. She researched cupboards and conference rooms, haughty brand-managers and under-appreciated finance specialists. There were 74 angry people in that building, 111 disillusioned, 56 remarkably naïve, and 12 beyond all reason. There was some overlap between categories.

One Wednesday, at the end of a hallway blocked by a dead dieffenbachia, Research found a staircase to the roof. Wednesday was the day of lowest absenteeism, on average. She pushed aside the plant, climbed the stairs, and thought about the researcher with his history of wok-fried bok choy and the other researcher with her hipless yet somehow voluptuous stride. She wanted to know how they were. She wanted her sex life to solve all the problems in her marriage. She wanted to fly in an airplane as if the sky were a grommet she could thread. She realized she was not going to get any of these things.

There was a small door at the top of the stairs that was obviously normally locked with a half-dozen padlocks and bolts, but was currently slightly ajar. She went out in the sunlight, seven stories closer to the sky then usual. A tiny silver jet arced above.

Various-sized metal boxes, wires, and poles were scattered over the tar-gravel rooftop. At one of the poles was the building services guy she knew – today his shirt said, "I know your Facebook password." He was scrabbling at a small metal box attached to the pole, twisting something inside it with a pair of pliers.

"Hello," she called.

The back beneath the thin shirt clenched. He turned, squinted into the sun.

"I'm from Research." She walked over. "I'd like to ask you some questions."

"What? Why?"

She picked her way over a few wires. "Why not? What are you doing?"

He shivered; seven stories made it windier. "Trying to fix the service disruption."

"Service disruption?"

"The Internet isn't working? For the whole building? Didn't you notice?"

"I haven't been online much lately. Nothing interesting." She shrugged. "What is your job?"

"Uhh . . ." she thought she saw blue light ream up his arm as he twisted the pliers, but he doggedly kept talking. He was, she realized, not much older than her sons. "Maintenance generalist."

"What do you . . ." Nothing seemed exactly imperative to know, with the wind and the sadness on the boy's face as he wrangled with the wires. One suddenly snapped and the end dropped below the box with another blue wave. And no one even knew he was up here, and everything seemed worth knowing. "What do you eat for lunch, most days?"

He knelt and gazed up at her. "Butternut squash soup, oftentimes. It comes in tetrapaks, $1.99 at No Frills. I heat it in the microwave, and buy a Jamaican patty from the cafeteria. And a Coke."

"Sounds good." She meant it, and meant to try it. "Also – "

More wires sproinged out of the box, seemingly spontaneously. The wind was picking up even more, but that couldn't have been why. He stood, pulling wires against his stomach as if his own intestines were escaping. "Do you have roof clearance?"

". . . I'm Research. I go everywhere."

"If you don't have clearance, you should probably – " he dropped his pliers.

" – could you please?"

She said, "I appreciate your time," but his face remained tight and nervous. So she went back to her ergonomic chair in the windless skyless research room. She ignored the red light of her voicemail. She was deleting emails unread when the phone rang.

"Hello, you've reached Research."

"Well, hellow there, young lady! Why doncha come down to our office to make your report? We've ordered in a pastry platter."

"Report?"

"There's fruit, too, if you're watching your weight."

"I didn't know . . . ."

"Of course not. You're very slender! But you know women . . . ."

"I – "

"Of course you know women! *The tongue is one of the strongest muscles in the body*! We've read the cunnilingus and airport notes that you saved to the server and we're *very* excited to hear more. So just you come on over to the executive wing, k?" Click.

She stared out the window where yet another plane from somewhere was careening out of the sky to nowhere. No, to Pearson International Airport, Mississauga. Mississauga was someplace. It was documented.

She took her notepads, her printouts from the Transit Authority and *Men's Health*. Bits of tar-gravel transferred from her shoes to the carpet as she walked.

Two men were sprawled on a couch in the executive suite. From the quarterly update meetings, she recognized them as the company's CEO and COO, Mark and Sanjeet. There was a tray of muffin halves and Danish slices on the desk. The sky outside the big executive window was dark. Yellow-green lights flashed at the airport. She wondered who had ordered the catering, who the caterers were, and where they ate their lunch. She wondered if she was in the mood for a carrot muffin.

Sanjeet clapped his hands together like thunder. "So! What's the report?"

Research said, "Many people in this company work very hard, eat healthfully, and keep their desks tidy."

"Yes!" said Mark. "Like you!"

"No, not like me. In different ways. There are many ways to do everything."

"In*deed!*" cried Sanjeet. "We are eager to know about the many paths, for example, to multiple orgasms. That article for *Dream Woman* was . . . powerful!"

"There is more to life than a carefully sucked clitoris," said Research, fact-checking herself as she spoke.

Mark's eyebrows lowered. "Of course. Like your airport research, very lofty. Were you sending it to *Dream Vacation*? Little thought-piece for the snowbirds?"

Research swayed. "There is a woman on the third floor who has memorized the photocopier manual. She works in logistics, but she has a small-machines certification. Everyone knows her, everyone calls her when the copiers bust. Her name is Marie."

The men looked, simultaneously, dismayed. "We employ a service company for those machines."

"Where are your notepads? How are you going to record what I'm telling you?"

A plane shuttled to the ground, red and yellow lights blinked, footsteps passed the door, a flash of conversation about "overseas workflows." The men said nothing.

"Yoghurt is the most popular snack food in this company. Even the lactose intolerant eat the soy stuff, like Katri at *Dream Romance*. Her favourite is raspberry."

"Aren't you interested in adventure, travel, pleasure?" Mark shoved half a raspberry Danish into her right hand.

"The airport is right there." She pointed at the window. "I see people travel all the time. But it doesn't have much to do with me."

Sanjeet shook his head. "We are Dream Magazines. Our magazines have nothing to do with the people who read them. That's what they like about them."

"It actually might not be. We don't know everything about everyone yet."

The windows in that office looked out onto thick purpling clouds, dancing with flecks of green lightning. She wondered who in the building had remembered an umbrella, who was unembarrassed to wear galoshes, and whose evening barbecue would be ruined by the rain. Sanjeet had just said something, but his mouth was full of muffin and she didn't quite get it – something about sexual freedom. She nodded, said, "Sounds fascinating." As soon as Research escaped this meeting, she could check the all the coathooks, whatever closets she could find, conduct an exit poll at the front door, and have rough estimates on all these rain matters by the end of the day. And then she could start the rest of her work.

To: All onsite employees
From: Social Committee
Re: Holiday Party

Friday 7:45 a.m.

Dear Dream Team,

It's November and you know what that means – many of you have missed the RSVP deadline for the Holiday Party. The deadline has now been extended until next Wednesday, but if you have not responded by then you will be UNABLE to do so, and therefore unable to attend the party.

Please note that you CANNOT RSVP by replying to this email – you MUST open the online form via the URL which was provided in your personalized invitation email. If you no longer have your invitation email you must contact a member of the Social Committee for it to be resent. You CANNOT use someone else's to respond to the invitation – the links are personalized and will save your dinner order (beef, fish, or vegetarian) and your guest's name.

Thank you for your cooperation,

The Social Committee

LONELINESS

THE CHIEF FINANCIAL OFFICER had something going on with one of the senior marketing managers. The fact that no one knew did not make the situation exactly comfortable for either of them, but it did make it manageable. They managed to smile pleasantly at each other over Styrofoam coffee in meetings, to hand each other brown plastic stir sticks. They managed to keep their public conversations restricted to profitable innovations in kitchen-cabinet refacing. They managed to keep the flirtation so low-key they almost did not notice it themselves. Or so either would've claimed, if asked. Neither was ever asked.

He did not work in Mississauga, in the Canadian branch office where she engineered pitches, sketched designs, wrote copy, took small uncatered meetings with subordinates who complained bitterly about substandard pens and lack of creative scope. He worked in head office, in a big American high-rise, in a vast and carpeted corner office where he could have had tapestries and sculpture, mounted fishes and trophies, or at least a couch and a minifridge, if he were so inclined. But he was not so inclined. Except for the Starbucks thermos, the photos of his kids, the extra ties and Rolaids, his office was as blank and impersonal as a model kitchen.

The American CFO's duties required him to come to the Canadian office only for quarterly presentations, and for years, so he did; Mississauga was only malls and Marriotts, and his children missed him. But then, one third-quarter close, his winter-chapped hand accidentally, absently, absorbedly brushed a wool-and-nylon thigh, and he began to find more conferences, more general

143

meetings and updates, worthy of his time. He began to accumulate Air Miles, and she stopped answering the smiles on Lavalife. He stopped phoning his ex late at night, and she started buying lingerie in candy colours.

The lingerie was theoretical; they had not even kissed. The silky pink camisole was something she slid into on mornings of ice-pellets and conference calls, something she wore under her sweater and touched sometimes, behind a door, in the restroom, her hand stealthily sliding up her own spine, alone.

Theirs was a flirtation of short emails and patchy cellphone calls. Once, a birthday card curled into a FedEx tube. Once – and nervously – lunch alone together in the employee cafeteria. Cheese cannelloni and diet Coke for both. Except for that first surreptitious caress of a thigh, several too-lingering arm-squeezes, and once when he held her coat for her and she, reaching backwards, missed entirely and stroked her palm down the flat expanse of his belly – except for these moments, there had been no physical contact at all.

Privately, they cursed themselves for teenaged fantasies that could, doubtless, lead only down alleys of frustration and masturbation. Desire only increases loneliness.

There had been moments of opportunity unrealized, when they were both perhaps stunned to realize their own limits. Both had attended a two-day trade show, sitting together at a particleboard demonstration, at a Kitchen of the Future demonstration, at an Ikea demonstration. They had sat together in the bar, and talked of the pets they had as children, animals now dead. They talked of their parents who were dead now, too, and how lonely it felt to walk the earth knowing their parents were dead. They talked about, or at least each somehow managed to mention, what their hotel room numbers were.

But someone joined them. Slouched towards each other on their bar stools, with hands loose on their beer steins, they looked only moderately engaged. A wet-looking sales rep joined them for some industry wisdom from the real actual CFO. This young man looked at the executives with the eyes of one coping with loneliness with a grim fire for professional advancement, warm only for ad sales, networking opportunities, firm handshakes.

The senior marketing manager could only leave gracefully, and she did. She went to her room knowing the number of his. It was 10:30 in the evening. He had a drink with the lost corporate soul, and then he went to his room knowing the number of hers. It was 11:09 in the evening.

To be in one's assigned room and then to go back into the hall felt like a heavy step on an avalanche-freighted mountain. Everyone knew that she was alone, he was alone, but at least they had their key-card doors to hide behind. To go out and wander the halls was an admission of loneliness rather than simply aloneness. Anyone seeing either of them padding down the hall would know this loneliness. Could that be borne?

She slid the chain and flipped back the bedspread and slid her palm at an angle between her thighs. He flipped the channels and sipped his tap water and looked for the porn not quite vivid enough to count as pay-per-view.

*

A declaration or confession begged to be made, lest energy that was as brilliant as single candle in a dark room go dead and dull as a flashlight. It is difficult to discern who finally took the point. Her, in lightly suggesting, into her flimsy silver phone, that he might attend the Canadian office's Holiday Soiree? She risked his awkward demurral, his too-loud laugh of apology. Or was the risk more his, for arranging the trip when his fellow executives thought it pointless and his children had hoped to ski? She said the entire company would like to see him there, plus he could see the social committee's accomplishment. He said it would be good for Canadian morale in these troubled economic times; his eldest son could be responsible for the car keys and grocery money.

Almost as strange as his RSVP was hers. To colleagues she said, why shouldn't she attend, though she hadn't in the seven years of employment? To herself she said, why shouldn't she wear a dress that plunged and glittered, though normally she shunned dresses that indulged in verbs?

Why shouldn't she sit next to him in the fir-strewn ballroom? There was no executive table; this was a free-thinking company, though generally executives liked to sit with executives, designers with designers, marketing staff with . . . But she sat with him, uninvited, except his wide-eyed glance across the ballroom, mid-conversation about real estate. Her colleagues and nearly-enough friends saw her drift past and sit far beyond the holiday tree. They said to each other that she would soon be promoted. She would be missed both in the office and at that dinner table, her arch chatter and penchant for drinking less than her share of the wine.

The CFO felt shame that the conversation he invited her into was only about housing prices, and would be for the entire evening, and there was nothing he could offer her, besides a compliment, and his napkin when hers fell to the floor. Only this.

He said to her, out of the corner of his mouth, "You look great," and she, without eye contact, having no real concept of what he was wearing, said, "You, too." The pink twist of his mouth, a touch of black-grey bristle missed by the razor, was all she watched.

There was a Portobello mushroom stack, a speech, supreme of chicken, speech, mango flan, speech and then the DJ took the podium and put on Bruce Springsteen. She whispered towards his shoulder, "Heaven help us – dancing."

They had to stay, since he at least had ostensibly crossed time zones for this celebration. But after having watched each other's mouths opening – parted lips, flash of teeth, slip of sautéed mushroom iridescent with butter – and closing – press of lips, the circular chew, slow clench of swallow – it was hard to sit quietly through the Jingle Bell Rock and the Macarena.

But he was from head office and she had her admirers and all would talk. So they talked, too, only occasionally with each other, and allowed wine, and then coffee, to be refilled. Their complicity was only that they did not allow themselves to be separated, drawn to distant tables, though several times they had to speak over each other.

So the evening went, as their lives had gone, colleagues, impressive wit, laughter, wine, but lurking at of the end of the evening, this one evening, perhaps something other than loneliness. Perhaps.

When she left, she smiled at him over her right shoulder (bare). He raised his mug (decaf, and he was embarrassed by it) and let someone who was no one in particular finish a sentence, and another two besides, before he followed her out.

She got her coat from the coat check and sat on a bench in the foyer that was secluded enough that she would not need to wave anyone goodbye. She thought she had probably made a mistake, imagined an opportunity where none existed or a protocol she could never know. She thought she would sit on the grey vinyl bench until she wilted, the spray-sheen evaporating from her hair, the perfect shade of blue from her dress, and the glow from her face. She would turn nothinger and nothinger, until there was eventually no need to drive herself home, because she could float, or fly, or not care where she was.

She was thinking about zooming through the brownish night sky over Toronto when the foyer doors swung open and he loomed grey-suited, coming towards her without seeing her. He had his right arm in his coat, the other sleeve trailing behind. This moment of imperfect communication – the anxious skitter of his gaze made clear he thought she'd left or was leaving – made her sad, for they really knew no more of each other than chatter and résumés and coffee cream. He didn't know if she'd issued the invitation or would want to, anymore than, until that moment, she knew if he'd seen it or cared.

And still in that crowded ballroom, she had tried to toss a flirtatious glance, despite her shelves full of Russian novels and closets full of orthopaedic shoes. And he had tried to accept it, despite his monochrome ties and fear of car mechanics. So she stood, and he saw her, and his gaze went smooth on her face, and he put on his other sleeve so he could offer her his arm.

It was late, it was dark, not many had stayed to the bitter battered end; perhaps no one saw them as they went through the parking lot to his rental car. She thought it best not to mention as they passed her snow-swaddled Prius. Perhaps they were seen and, in other cars, commented upon, laughed at for their prim middle-aged debauchery, their weak defenses against loneliness. She felt only the inside of his forearm over the inside of her forearm. But for two coats, his suit jacket and dress shirt and her moisturizer – but for all that, touch.

It was only when the engine was warming and seatbelts were buckled that he said, "I will drive you home," and she said, "Yes."

Her home was a condo on the southern hem of the city and she had wanted it desperately until she first slept there, high and expensive, drifting over the lake, dreaming of mortgage payments.

He didn't really know the city, didn't know on-ramps, exit signs, and had no internal compass to know west, east, lake, city. She had to direct him, and thought briefly that the dull maritalness of "You're going to want to get over, it's a left merge," would dim the thing that had been sharp and glittering in the air between them all evening, all year, always.

But her voice seemed to him bellish and clearish and dimmed nothing. He wished he didn't need directions, he wished he had somehow practiced this beforehand, but to indicate turns she touched the inside of the elbow, warm through all those layers of cloth.

Idling outside the condo tower when she said, "Here, right here," he suddenly felt a whirl of inexperienced years, marriage and before, always. What did he say, what did he assume and deliberately not say? Exhaust fumed into the gutter and the eyes of cats. He said, one thousand years old, feeling like a child, "I hate to – Would you . . . could I come up for a while?"

She might have, just might have, rolled her eyes, but he caught it only in the rearview and couldn't be sure. That hand on his arm again, eyes full of . . . something less ironic. She handed him a blank plastic card. She said the magic words, "Visitor parking is underground."

When he parked badly and babbled on, when she couldn't find her key and babbled on, when there was nothing in the world to say in the elevator, they were both embarrassed, and united in this.

It was a relief to be inside her modest white condo, their chilled feet curling into the modest pile of the living room carpet. It was a relief to do something, at last, that was wordless, was only themselves.

No.

It wasn't *only*, nor wordless. Even as they walked sock-footed towards each other on the carpet, each remembered that night in words, in the language of a self-told story that each would tell silently against the cold loneliness of future nights, all the nights that might ever come. Their memories were words.

Even as she rocked against him she was remembering how he tucked her weight into him. She remembered. Even at his first shock at how cold her lips were – how could they have chilled inside his warm rental car? – he remembered the warm-cool, the pressure, her hand on his arm.

But she did warm up and he pulled her in tighter and it became a moment where they wondered what came next. He wondered how to ask where her bedroom was. He wondered if that was to ask too much, to imply he'd spend the night when the living room floor seemed much more one-night-stand-ish. His hand cupped the outside of her left breast almost unsuccessfully, so thoroughly was that breast cupped by her strapless padded underwire bra, which was almost all he felt. But still he felt her a little, too, soft and thrilling. He had never had a one-night stand; the protocol could have been anything.

She didn't want to make love on the carpet, under the ceiling light from Restoration Hardware, their limbs tangled and cold, backs twisting and spasming. She didn't know if he'd ever looked closely at her eyes or her waist or her job description, but she was a *senior* marketing manager, and it showed in all the ways she bent gently in yoga class, sat down to take off her boots, made love in the dark.

And so she tugged his tie and took his hand on down the condo-sized hallway. The bed was perfectly made, for she had expected, hoped, something. And then there they were.

He unzipped her dress. He knew how to do it in a long graceful sweep; he had been married for something. He'd always admired the silvery sound of a gown splitting open.

The fabric fell away from her fast, too fast, she hadn't realized she would be bared so quickly and the duvet still tucked in. She felt the whoosh at her knees and, before he could look down, she pressed herself tightly to him, her nylon hips a jolt, bra cups crumpling, ripples of stomach invisible.

He was startled, pleased by her ardency and also by the pressure of her lingeried body against him. She kissed his mouth, to keep up the show of passion that was becoming fact, slowly, nearly, anyway. She slid her palms up his dress shirt, past the droplet of red wine beside the navel, the smear of butter beneath his left nipple. She slid her hands under the silky (not silk) lining of his jacket and up over his rounded, unmuscled shoulders.

He let his arms go slack, and heard his dry-clean-only jacket crumple to the floor. Immediately fingertips to bra-clasp. As if to make up for every high-school fumble in the dark, the hooks uncoupled easy as breath, and in another instant the tip of her clay-dark nipple brushed the butter stain. He thought of the bun he'd dropped, then eaten anyway. Soft, white and sweet.

Both were aching, damp and hot, tangled in her bra strap and his tie, waiting. Finally, he pulled back impatiently, yanking his tie and toeing off his socks simultaneously. She, bereft, underwire-less and seven pounds above her ideal BMI, dove underneath the fluffy white duvet.

She watched his chest appear (the tie was on the floor by the time she was covered) from the stained shirt. He regretted the white hairs sprigging through the chestnut, the paunch of ice cream in front of the TV; she didn't. He unbuckled his belt. It didn't make that rattling sound that she thought all male belts made.

While he undid the button hidden cleverly in the fabric at the top of his fly, she squirmed a hand under her pantyhose at the centre of her belly, more imitation than self-stimulation. She rolled down the waistband as he slid his slacks to the floor. She was writhing under the covers to free her feet as he rounded the bed, eager now without the chaste pale cotton boxers. He was also raw with visibility, though, wanting to touch her partly so she'd stop watching him.

She doubled underneath the duvet to remove her flesh-toned, flesh-shaping, unerotic panties, kicking them out the far side of the bed. When she emerged, he was beside her and she reached up and the duvet slid down and he saw her breasts and they were beautiful, and then he pressed on top of her and she flattened out beneath him and her beautiful breasts gritted on his perfect grey-and-chestnut chest hair. He pressed his mouth to the curve below her ear, and his penis to the curve below her stomach, and she kissed his hair and rubbed against his hip, and they were like that for a long time. His tongue in her mouth in hers in his. His palm at her ribcage, his fingers on her shoulder blades.

Suddenly, perfectly, in nearly a single movement, they both drew back, rolled apart, her reaching for the box in the bedside drawer, him scrambling into the chill of the room for his wallet twisted in his pants. Both thought warmly, dreamily, of the naïve and hopeful fools they'd been that afternoon, averting their eyes while setting down condom packets in front of jaded cashiers in two Shoppers Drug Marts miles apart. They'd both bought the same brand, though they would never know.

They used hers. She kissed his throat, belly, hip, foreskin, before all the steps of squeezing out air and rolling rubber gently down. They would never know each other's dead parents, he would never meet her estranged sister, she would never befriend his rebellious furious children; they could only have so much and even then they knew it.

Slicked, sheathed, *safe*, he looked at her eyes and didn't feel safe. He felt a spiral of vertigo, because her eyes could've been hazel or navy in that dim room, and he didn't know but wanted to be inside her with a longing that covered any colour her eyes could possibly be, all the flavours of yoghurt and religious practices and arguments with her sister and work-life imbalances and ugly bathing suits she could ever consider. He was scared he knew nothing about her and would want her under any circumstances.

She lay on the sheets where she had been with men she didn't take her bra off for, or even her blouse, once, and she had been meek and casual as they left in the dark. It was a bland pale room and he improved it, his crumpled charcoal pants and hairy unsmooth chest and the clinkless belt and the unjoined earlobes swinging free, her genetic opposite. She wanted to absorb it all, hair and finance and suavity at parties and awkwardness in cars. She wanted to devour his driver's license.

He slipped inside her, she slipped inside him, their stomachs tight and slick together.

It could never be put into words, what they desired.

She said his name, loudly, an almost-wail as they began to move. He clutched her and said her name.

These were the words they said, all they could say to cover each other that night and the nights that would come after, if any ever could.

DREAM INC.

SANJEET WAS LOST in a tangle of bodies and mist from dry ice and sweat and terrible music. The male vocalist whined that everyone should wave their hands around, the drum machine sounded aggressively unlike a drum, and Sanjeet finally spotted Mark. The chief executive officer of Dream Inc. Canada was leaning against a wall in a fire-exit hall at the back of the club. The flash off the disco ball illuminated his face pale and silvery. Sanjeet stood a good distance away, at the mouth of the hall, but he could see that Mark's eyes were closed.

The young woman at the CEO's feet had long slippery straight hair – he couldn't make out the colour, because every flash from the main room dyed it green or purple. She was looking up at Mark's face from waist-level while she pushed her hair back and, Sanjeet could have sworn, wiped her mouth. After a moment, without Mark opening his eyes, she grabbed his limp hand and pulled herself up. Her tiny skirt revealed a silver thong and a purple-flash ass.

By the time Sanjeet reached the couple, the music had changed to jagged rap over the same fake drum and the girl was tucked in close to Mark's pink-shirted chest (Sanjeet wondered what had happened to his chalk-stripe suit jacket). She was still clutching his hand. Mark might have been sleeping. The girl glanced at Sanjeet. Her lips gleamed when the light hit them – it could have been lip gloss, but Sanjeet was worried it was semen. He and Mark had a close working relationship, one that included the occasional too-much-party vomit, but never semen.

"Mark!"

His eyes opened, quicker than Sanjeet expected. "What?"

There were a million whats – leading the pack, what they would say in the "directional" meeting with their American parent-company's leadership first thing in the morning – but suddenly he felt as if he'd shown up in Mark's bedroom instead of the fire-exit hallway of an ugly club. "I'm going," he said finally.

"What?"

He jerked his thumb at the door. "Seeya back at the hotel." He took a step following his thumb.

"Going?" Mark grabbed his shoulder, digging like a crab-claw.

The girl gazed from one man to the other.

"Yeah, we got that thing in the morning, and then the flight . . . ." Sanjeet had hit on like 14 women, dancing well, smiling well, and gotten nowhere. At least he hadn't lost *his* jacket. He wanted to go back to the hotel and drink the minibar and sleep and wake up and have an entire plate full of bacon at the breakfast buffet. Then get to work.

Mark squirmed away from the female, staggered deeply and grabbed her bare shoulder for support. "If yer gonna go, um unna go too." He turned to peer into the girl's face. "Whirr in*sepa*rable. Bess . . . colleagues. He goes, I gotta go. Yah unnerstand?"

"Yeah, that's nice." She reached up and squeezed the hand on her shoulder, and then tugged it off. "Bye." She turned down the hall to a door marked Fire Exit. No alarm bells went off when she went out.

Sanjeet turned to watch her go and then Mark threw his arms around his shoulders, leaning his full weight against his back. When Sanjeet twisted back, they were closer than they'd ever been before. "Are you really this drunk? Or were you roofied?"

Mark pressed his face into Sanjeet's shoulder. "I am this grunk," he muttered through a mouthful of expensive fabric. "Are we really going to lose the company?"

The music had become a female moan. "I – " Sanjeet pulled Mark's left arm until it was around his own shoulders, then began hauling him through the club " – am not drunk enough for this conversation."

*

They slept in and missed the breakfast buffet, and the meetings were grim, endless, and uncatered. Of course, O'Hare was a hot mess, as always – their flight was an hour delayed, the guy who checked their baggage was visibly holding back tears, and there was a pigeon in the foyer. They had some sort of business airline membership that entitled them to sit in a sealed-off glass room with comfortable chairs and drink tepid imported beers, but that was useless at eleven a.m. when you were hungry. Those lounges always had bits of cheese and grapes that were deflated on the underside. They went to a restaurant anyone could go to, instead.

Sanjeet read the menu as Mark muttered into his phone at his wife – Sanjeet could hear Devorah's squeaky snarl in between Mark's words. "Yes, we are. I said *yes*. No. Terrible. I really – don't want to go into it. I said *no*. K, goodbye. *Jesus*. I love you too."

There was quiet music playing – while Mark redialed you could hear it. It had some sort of chimes and a heavy bass, haunting but tinny and faint. It took him a minute to locate the source – a laptop on the next table, guarded by a dark-haired woman bent so low over her work you couldn't even see if she was pretty. The lyrics – now that he was focused he could hear them – were about hanging around wearing bathing suits, but the low slow music was so dark. When she glanced up, he still couldn't peg her attractiveness, obscured by glasses and hair and the flush of finding him watching. She bent again and plugged in her earphones and he lost access to the sound and her face.

All morning, throughout his thoughtful recitation of their company's woes, through the insistence of head-office that the

Canadian team fold one of their major magazines and outsource the call centre – through it all, Mark had been hungover miserable and Jeet had carried him. But now they were alone, together, the flight was delayed, it was eleven a.m. on a Thursday, the restaurant wasn't even serving breakfast, and Mark was listening to the refracted ring on his inane wife's bejeweled Blackberry Pearl.

"She doesn't want to hear you say goodbye again. Put it away." When Mark did, Sanjeet started immediately with, "I can't believe that with all this shit yesterday, overhead cuts and layoffs and looking like idiots, we take a break to get politely trashed and you not only forget to call Devorah, you find your second wind to fuck a teenager." He took a breath as the waitress arrived. She was obviously herself a teenager and wide-eyed at these flabby, bedheaded, unshowered gentlemen in smoke-coloured suits wishing to fuck her. She set down the coffees.

"Thanks." Mark took a gulp, winced. "Could we have some cream? And eggs?"

"I *told* you, sir, the breakfast stops at ten."

"Oh. Yeah."

The girl continued to stare, bellicose but uncertain too. "You ordered the chicken burger. Do you still want that?"

Mark's glossy black Boss shirt was three buttons undone, revealing chest hair. "Um, sure."

"Ok." She turned away slowly, as if they might jump her.

"To return to the topic at hand . . ." said Sanjeet.

Mark blinked hard. "To return to the topic at hand . . . what? We went to dinner, we went to that *stupid* club with the Australians – if there's any national heads in worse shape than us it's them. Ok, I got more than what *you'd* call 'politely' trashed, but you're a born-again virgin, these days."

Sanjeet's scalp crinkled in rage, but Mark kept talking. "And then back to the hotel to sleep it off. I don't remember every detail but I know I didn't . . ."

"Didn't get a blowjob in the back hallway from a 19-year-old?"

A bowl of dairy cuppets hit the table hard, and a two-percent bounced out. "Here you go!" It was hard to tell if the edge to the waitress's voice was nerves or rage.

"Thank you." Sanjeet scooped up the milk before it rolled off the table.

She gave them a grim, appraising look before leaving.

Mark said slowly, almost hopefully, "I don't even remember hitting on anyone. I mean, I don't do that, right?" He tapped the phone.

Sanjeet sighed, peeled back the milk top and poured it into Mark's coffee. "Congratulations. Do you remember *anything*, though? If the whole evening's blank, I don't know how much you can really assert . . . ."

"I remember . . . music, dancing. I danced with that marketing lady . . . Pam?"

"Ok, the girl I saw kneeling by your dick did not look like she was from the direct-marketing division."

"*Kneeling by my* – ? So where *did* she look like she was from?"

"High school."

Mark smiled. "That doesn't sound like me . . . ."

Sanjeet rolled a creamer in his fingers. "Fine. You fucked a teenager when you were too drunk to remember it. You're 45, but I guess as the head of a foundering magazine concern, about to be sold for parts by the parent company, that's about right . . . ."

"Even if what you said is true, I didn't *fuck* her. A blow job . . ."

"I believe the technical term is *face-fucking*."

"Weren't we born in the same year?" Mark slumped forward as the waitress arrived with the chicken burger and pizza. She thumped them down, then departed. "Aren't you COO of that same failed concern?"

"Oh, I know. We have to reach a 30% reduction in head count, make a restructuring plan."

Mark picked up his burger. "The other was more interesting. But ok, let's work."

Sanjeet held his fork up. "Is this a pepperoni?"

"I would assume so, yes. That's the logical circular meat to find on a pizza."

"I ordered plain. I'm vegetarian this week. It's like a mini-cleanse."

"Man, you just can't win. So, we gotta outsource the CSRs?"

Sanjeet pressed the fork tines against the edge of his plate until the meat slid off. "So you've heard nothing that's been said the last 18 hours, is what you're saying?"

Mark reached for the leather file folder lying on the table. "I'm here now, man."

*

Sanjeet liked his commute. When he was doing his MBA and living on soba, when he and Mark were putting together their first scrappy-weird fashion mag and working 17 hours a day, he had pictured a lot of things about his future, but not the crush of the 401 as the sun rose behind him, tinting his dashboard gold and fuchsia. This had never been the status symbol he'd had in mind: a dull silver Mercedes stuck in traffic for 45 minutes as Kelly Clarkson gasped along with the string section. Still, it was nice. Satellite radio pre-sets, expensive Free Trade coffee in a stainless steel coffee mug – these were the little signs that a life was working out pretty goddamned well.

What he didn't like was the way the problems of the upcoming infringed upon the drive. It was supposed to be just him and Kelly and his coffee, all the way from the loft by the water to the sprawling Mississauga parking lot of Dream Inc. But when he was fretting about how pissed the laid-off people were going to be, he was not savouring the traffic and sky and coffee. The fretting was like the music – the second he silenced the radio, that dark grimy tune from the restaurant-girl's laptop was droning in his head. He didn't like not being able to control his internal pre-sets.

At work, Sanjeet was rounding the corner to the exec wing when he couldn't resist glancing into HR – another pre-set he hadn't chosen. Belly's big clean office faced the hall, and she sproinged up from her ergonomic chair when she saw him. Her silk blouse tightened against her chest in the wind of her stride. Her briskness was only somewhat undercut by the fact that her shoes made no sound.

"Welcome back. You missed some things. How did it go?"

"Thanks. What things? Terrible."

"A girl fell down the east stairwell and broke her leg. We have a mouse infestation and they've been chewing through the phone jacks. And there was some kind of scuffle in Customer Service yesterday – huge mess."

"Ah. So, you haven't been running the company all that well in our absence."

Belly drew herself up. "What happened?"

They walked down the wide bright hallway in silence. Sanjeet wondered where the art on the walls had come from – there was one of a nude turned away in blue and purple shadows, another of a puppy staring quizzically at the viewer. He liked them all.

"Is it really that bad, Jeet? Or are you just not allowed to tell me?"

"It's . . . it's bad, Belly. Maybe you *should* run the company. We're gonna outsource the customer service team, and *Dream Woman* is gonna fold. And then . . . we can hold on for a while."

"Even worse than the mice." Belly flopped onto the leather couch in his office, which made a *whoomp* noise as the air shot out. "But what about all the staff issues at *Dream Condo*? What about the mess with art and design? What did they say about that stuff?"

"We didn't ... we didn't go over every single issue. The parent-company guys, they have a dozen international outfits, a hundred publications. We did the big stuff."

He realized Mark was behind them by the noise of his mastication. He turned as a fat cranberry fell out of Mark's muffin onto the steel-grey carpet. "He lives!"

"Hello, darling. What's for dinner?"

Mark thrust the muffin at him and Sanjeet took a big bite without using his hands.

"You guys are hilarious," said Belly, trying to put her hands on her hips while sunk in the couch. "You're really going to let all of customer service go?"

"You say *you* like it's our brilliant idea. This is coming from head office. They have some great deal in Chennai for the American mags, so they're trying it . . . ."

Belly looked at Mark. "Is there a muffin tray?"

"No, I just got this for myself at Coffee Time. Sorry."

She sighed. Mark and Sanjeet chewed. Finally Mark swallowed and cleared his throat. "So, you'll get on it?"

"On what?"

"On the layoffs, Belly, can you arrange the paperwork?"

"Right away?" Her voice was bright, but her jaw clenched. They stared at her; Belly was usually ironically put-upon, but this time there was something else.

"This has got to be as soon as possible, the notice and the severance and everything, so the new team can start up."

"Yeah." She shrugged. "Gotta be."

Sanjeet tipped his head back against the wall above the couch. His eyes were shut but he felt the couch lower then rise when she stood.

*

After Belly left, Sanjeet realized he was sweating through the collar of his lavender dress shirt. "She didn't sound too hop-to-it," he said, struggling out of his jacket.

"Hop?" Mark muttered as if just waking.

"The layoffs? Symonds said we should – " he made curly-fingered quotation marks " – *hop to it.*" More quotation marks.

Mark sat up and looked Sanjeet in the eyes. "I'm a good person."

Sanjeet rubbed the fronts of his thighs. "Sure."

"I still don't really remember but I am sure I just wouldn't have. Not with a – Christ, if she were 18, I'm almost two-and-a-half times that."

"I'm the ops guy, I'll do the math." Sanjeet flipped open his portfolio and sucked something out of his molar. "Apparently, our inbound *and* outbound call-scripts suck."

"You don't believe me."

"I have no interest in what you said. That can't be called belief or non-belief."

"You care. Jeet, I saw, yesterday in the Denny's – you were disgusted with me."

"No. You're my CEO. You get your dick out in public and the wrong people take an iPhone pic, I'm in almost as much shit as you. But I don't *judge* you. Also, that was not a Denny's." The song in his head was just a couple bars on endless repeat – he couldn't remember the words or even most of the melody. Maddening.

"Bullshit."

"Denny's does not have a franchise in O'Hare airport. I would – "

"Bullshit, 'I don't judge, I just think you are a tabloid headline waiting to happen.' If you weren't such a prude – "

"I really don't think it's repressed – what are we talking about? How do you make your sex life take precedence over people getting fucked in a way that actually matters?"

"I don't."

"Do you think any of customer service cares about your *issues* when they're not going to be getting cheese on their burgers for the next while?"

Mark inhaled deeply through his nostrils. "Ok, ok, right. I'm being ridiculous. Over something that maybe, *probably* didn't even happen. What do we have to do?"

"For the layoffs, actually, not much. It's a Belly thing – an HR thing. We just need to think about what's next in terms of editorial, and decide – "

Mark swallowed the last bit of muffin. "We should plan some remarks . . . ."

"I don't think . . . I don't think so."

"I'm a good person." Mark's lower lip stuck out slightly.

"You think no one ever got laid off before?"

"Not by me."

*

Mark's earnest speech on accountability and acknowledging errors won over Sanjeet. Belly was tougher, concerned that their presence would tempt laid-off employees to assign blame, get hostile. They had promised to follow her script to the letter.

Belly explained that the best time to do these things was nine a.m. Studies showed that people felt stupid for working all day not knowing that it was for nothing. So they all had to come in early on Tuesday to prepare for all those workdays that wouldn't be.

They were using the HR meeting room, not the CSR one, for a reason Belly had explained but Sanjeet forgotten. He liked to think it was because that people were more reserved in unfamiliar territory. Why he broke up with women in parks and malls.

It had taken two weeks to get to this point in the layoff process, and yet Sanjeet still had that damn sad song in his head. It was the soundtrack as Mark wandered in carrying a briefcase though he usually had a courier bag and usually left that in his office.

"Where's the catering?"

"No catering. This is a short, focused meeting – no mingle-muffin time," Belly snapped without looking up from her folder.

"I feel like – " Mark dropped the briefcase heavily " – we should at least give'em breakfast. So they're ahead on that front, you know. One less meal to buy?"

"I do not think an 80-cent muffin will put them very far ahead. But you can go to the caf and ask if it's too late to set up a tray. If you want." Belly was wearing an emerald green blazer, as if she had just won the Masters, but sexier, with a silky white blouse. It should not have been sexy at all, but it was. The blouse was probably not even real silk.

A head popped into the doorway. Pale with blond cropped hair like a soldier. "Is this where the CSR update is?"

Belly straightened, which had the effect of thrusting out her breasts. "Yes. But not for half an hour."

The guy nodded. He was wearing a greyed white button-down and dark jeans – clearly the last rung of business-casual. "Cool, I'll hang out in here, cause the CSR room is locked for some reason. Is there muffins?"

Belly's eyes bugged. "Actually – no, no muffins. And we need the room." The guy jerked back slightly. "Sorry. We're just . . . could you wait in the cafeteria, please?"

"Oh. Ok." He backed out slowly, gaze lingering on the table at the front of the room, as if the muffins might appear there. Then he was gone.

Belly clomped over to shut the door. At least she was wearing shoes that made a sound. "Shit. I told building services to box the department this after*noon*."

Sanjeet glanced at Mark. "Should I check in with the new call centre?"

Mark nodded, then shook his head. His hair needed a cut; it flopped like Hugh Grant's. "I got it covered. Well, Shulman and I do. The guys in Chennai come online today at nine a.m. our time. They did a training session last week. It's all easy. And cheap."

"You arranged all this without my input? Isn't this more of an operations thing?"

"It would seem that letting the old team go would be your implicit consent to having a new team start. Or were you planning on just letting the phone ring?"

"You just should have involved me."

Mark sat in a folding chair. "We're in a bad spot. I'm trying to improve things."

Sanjeet slid down the wall until he was poised as if sitting in a chair. He knew it was an exercise his trainer recommended, but he couldn't recall the name. The song in his head was a kind of looping swirl, and it was starting to give him a headache. "It's not a 'spot.' We haven't met any of our financial targets, operating costs are way up, circulation's tanking and staff is heading to the competition. This company isn't going to be ours much longer. If it exists at all."

"That's not the take-away I got from the head-office dudes in Chicago."

Sanjeet sank lower, onto the floor. "If you weren't busy fucking teenagers, you would've – "

"I didn't fuck her!" Mark stood, towering over Sanjeet.

"Fine, face-fucked then. Is the technical term."

"Je*sus.* I'm *here*, guys." Belly waved her brightly manicured hand and, when the men just stared at her, added quietly, "I've outlined the issues with overhead – "

"An overhead projector? What is this, grade 5 geography class?"

"Would you *listen*? I was going to say, the overhead *costs* making it difficult to maintain an in-house customer service team." She paused and blinked rapidly, then kept talking. "There'll be time for your remarks after that. Stick to your script, or legal will have an aneurysm. I'll have the packages by the door. It'll be awkward – people have to say their names and wait while I flip through. I'm gonna get Kat helping, but it'll – "

Sanjeet said, "Cat?"

"*Kat,* my assistant. C'mon, Jeet, get up and focus. This is the worst day of a lot of other people's lives, but not yours."

Sanjeet shook his head, then nodded. "Yeah. Yes. Ok." He struggled to his feet, wondering if it was clear to Belly that it was *Mark* engaged in the fuckery, not himself. He couldn't think how to clarify. The silence felt thick and spreading.

The door opened again and people began coming in. They were mainly quite young – some looked like high school students. One looked like Mark's club girl, only without the flashing green and purple. The moment Sanjeet spotted her kneeling in the hall, her mouth had been open because she'd been laughing, a small wry laugh. She had been shockingly lovely. Sanjeet never had a blow job from, or even been touched by, someone like that.

Mark and Belly were at the front of the room, sorting thick folders on a table. Sanjeet hadn't noticed the dangling green earrings before – she was really trying. She must have thought her job was in danger too. Belly wasn't stupid.

Sanjeet got up and headed for the door, nodding sharply at Mark, who followed. Belly put her hand up, fingers splayed, mouthing what was probably *five minutes.*

In the hallway, Mark leaned against the wall and held out some pages. "Take a look at this? I knew Belly's notes would be all legal crap, so I whipped this up."

"If we go off-script, *then* we'll have the legal crap – Belly's the one that memorized the Employment Standards Act, not us." But he was already reading. "This might go over. Maybe *value the contributions of each and every one of you* is too much?"

"What, we don't?"

"Yeah, no, just *each and every one* is a little – Tiny Tim, you know?"

The building was fuller now; people occasionally brushed between them, smiling carefully. When they were alone again for a moment, Sanjeet began reading aloud: "A job is a time in life, a period of efforts and colleagues, successes and disappointments. We applaud your efforts during your time at Dream Inc. and wish you all success wherever you next apply your efforts." He tipped his head to the side. "It's pretty good. Philosophical – lets them put it a bit into perspective."

"That's what I meant. I mean, this feels like a big deal, but it's just the end of a thing, which is how all new things start." He squinted down the corridor towards design. A woman with dark bobbed hair and large breasts pressing against her plain white blouse was approaching.

Belly's amber-and-honey-streaked head ducked into the hall. "Showtime, guys."

"Uh." Jeet waved the papers absently. "Just give us a moment more."

Belly pulled a strand of hair from her mouth, ready to speak, but someone called from behind her. She rolled her eyes, then vanished.

The breasty woman passed, nodded at them, wafted a breeze of grain and sugar – the oatmeal muffin from the caf? Her retreating form was of a wide ass in a narrow grey skirt. Sanjeet muttered, "There's a new thing to start."

"Well."

"*Well*? She was better than your blowjob cheerleader? Did you see that ass?"

"Did you see that *ring*?" Mark said.

"Ah, it's marriage that matters now."

"You're not going to *tell* Devorah anything, right? About this thing that maybe didn't even happen?"

Sanjeet tried to imagine his dick and a woman like the one who had just passed and found it a little sexy but mainly repellant. He was pleased to find that a ring would mean something to him, despite that taut expanse of tweed skirt. "I try not to talk to Devorah about anything at all."

Mark tipped his head back. "I don't remember, but I can imagine. It's too easy to imagine for it not to have happened. So it probably did. I totally dropped the ball on those new contracts, drowned my sorrows in bad liquor, and fucked a teenager to cheer myself up, thus breaking my marriage vows. And blacked out. Classy."

"Face-fucked, remember. Or don't remember."

"I'm the kind of slobbering old dirtbag the girls used to make fun of in university."

"Oh, we're all that, now."

Belly poked out her head again, earrings swinging. Her usual ironic squint was widened, which had the effect of making her sharp nose look beaky – she was suddenly much less attractive than usual. "Guys, we better . . . I don't think I should stall anymore."

Jeet tried to nod thoughtfully. "We just need another minute."

"You *had* five minutes." In this focused mode, Belly's long-lashed blink was not as sexy, and thus not as threatening, as usual.

For once, he was able to dismiss her. "Just a *minute,* Belly." The door shut on Belly's alto sigh and that song was back in his head, that thrum. He started to mutter, "Something-something bathing-suits, something torture . . ."

Mark's head jerked around sharply – he had been peering down the hall after that magnificent ass. "Is that a *song?*"

"It was playing on that chick's laptop, in the airport restaurant? Remember?"

"No. What?"

Sanjeet fished his iPod out of his hip pocket. "I have it." There was no response, so he kept on talking. "It's a really weird song, but I dunno, I like it. Took me forever to google the right lyrics to get a title, figure out the band, download it, whole bullshit . . . ."

"There's an app for that, you know. It's – "

"I *know*. I just didn't think of it at the time." He slid his thumb around the click wheel.

"Is that a new one? I thought you had a green one?"

"This one is green. It just looks bluish in this fluorescent light."

"No, but a long skinny one?"

"Oh, yeah, I *did* have one of those, but that was ages ago." He continued to click, as the door opened again.

"We'll just be – " Sanjeet turned to see not Belly in the doorway, but the pale low-slung boy who had wanted a muffin. He shuffled quickly past, clutching a blue folder to his chest. Another boy, bigger and older but still not a man, followed, also with a folder. After him was a pretty girl, young enough that her freckles stood out on her face like markered dots. And after her was a whole roomful more.

To: All onsite employees; temps and contractors;
sales staff
From: Mark Harlan-James
CC: Sanjeet Rafeal
Re: Customer Service Department

                                    Friday 9:45 a.m.

Dear Dream Team,

Please note that our Customer Service functions have
been transferred to the FirstLook sales team. Working
from a large, modern office in Chennai, India, FirstLook
has built a solid reputation for service, care, and
professionalism, and we are very pleased to be working
with them.

    The new team will be headed by Waheeda
Venkatesan. Any questions or concerns should be
forwarded to Belinda Martin, VP Human Resources, who
will answer or forward to Waheeda as necessary.

We look forward to a long and prosperous relationship
with the folks at FirstLook.

Cheers,
Mark and Sanjeet and all of the Executive Team

THIS WEATHER
I'M UNDER

TONIGHT, EVEN IF it doesn't stop raining, even if I haven't yet found those lost files for customer service, I will leave the office before the cleaning staff arrives. I will shut down my computer before I hear the crash of their cart full of recyclables catching the hallway rug, the way it does every night. I will shut down my computer, take my trenchcoat from the hook, and drive to the hospital.

I want to get to there for the start of visiting hours, but I also want to avoid the awkwardness of watching the cleaners work. As VP of Human Resources, I am well aware that staff don't like to feel over-supervised. As a hotel guest who once tried to help the chambermaid make my bed, I know they resent it. When I got into bed that night the sheets were tucked in so tight, I was pinned flat to the mattress.

So I have just a few minutes to find some evidence in our computer system that the call-centre staff actually works here. Somehow, despite the documentation protocols I enforce, the customer service "Personnel Info" folder is nearly empty. There has to be more than six of them answering all our incoming calls. I could have sworn there was a big black guy in that group – I've seen him in meetings – yet no such picture appears in the org chart. Even if people left, there still would be files in the "Former" folder. Anyway, they must still work here because the reason I have to find them is to lay them off.

We don't just lose people at Dream Inc. This is a big office, but we keep track of things. Of people. The people are my job. My mother taught me to keep track of things and has always been proud that I was made VP HR at a vibrant national magazine company when I was only 39. I'm 42 now, and Dream is not as vibrant as it once was, and my mother sometimes needs assistance breathing. But life goes on and so does work. I will go see her as soon as I have found the files on the dozen or so customer-service reps that I almost know exist, and once it stops raining.

But they aren't in a backup folder, and they aren't filed with the sales team, so I start jotting down names I think I recall, but then I hear the recycling-cart crash – resolution failed. And then my phone rings; not the desk phone, the real one in my purse. Mainly work people call me on it when I am not here, but so do other people: eHarmony dates from three months ago, drunk and wondering if they'll ever have kids; offers for cruise vacations with fog horns blowing in the background. And sometimes my stoic sister, Desi, in muted hysteria because my mother has fallen down in the Food Basics parking lot, or keeps talking to the nurse's aid as if he's her dead husband. Or is having trouble breathing. Or more trouble. Or has been hospitalized. Or is in surgery. She could call for another reason, but she hasn't, yet. I exist in a state of readiness.

Except the purse strap is stuck in the drawer, jamming it shut, and I hate my pretty red Steve Madden bag. I'm on my knees by the time I finally yank open the drawer, then the bag, and rummage through parking receipts and dead pens to find the phone.

The screen says *Desi*. "Hello? What's up?"

"Yeah, easy tiger. You ok?"

"Nothing wrong?"

"Many things wrong, but nothing new. Well, you're not here. She wants you. Where are you?"

"Work. I'm coming in just – "

There's a shifting sound, and when I peek above my desk, the cleaning woman is above me, reaching for the wastebasket. "Oh!" she shrieks. "Are you ok?"

"I'm fine." I smile encouragingly at her, then at the waste-basket.

"Great, see you soon." Nothing fazes Desi.

The woman above me is fazed though. "Oh. I'll come back." I have never been able to figure out her accent, though I hear the cleaners yelling up the hall almost every night. Wherever they are from, I'm pretty sure they're from the same place.

"No, I'm going." I squirm up into my chair and reach for the keyboard. "I've just got to – " I had about seven documents open and when I try to close them all, the screen freezes. "You can go ahead and start vacuuming or whatever." I click Start, I hit crtl-alt-del, nothing. I try to think if I had anything unsaved, whether my mom is alert enough to notice if I don't visit tonight, how pathetic it is trying to learn about the men and women of customer service so I can do the layoff paperwork. The cleaning woman watches.

I reach for the power button, but even that is impotent. The woman has not begun to clean. A male voice hollers down the hall in Czech or Tagalog for all I know. The woman turns towards the voice, but all she says is "No!" Then she turns back. "Vacuum? You have a spill, a mess?" She sounds like my mother, or some-body's mother, anyway.

"No, no mess." I crouch back down under the desk, flick the green power-bar button, and hear the moan of shutdown. When I pop my head over the top of the desk, the woman looks terrified. "If you weren't going to vacuum tonight, that's fine, too."

"We . . . don't mainly. Just if there is a big spill. But the vac-uum is in the car. You want me get?"

That's her first grammatical error since we've been talking. I straighten up; I must look crazy peering at her from half-under the desk. "Sure, no, you can just . . . what do you need to do?" I am certain they never dust; all my papers and Post-its and Kinder Surprise toys are always as I left them, and the dust too.

The woman draws herself up. She isn't young or old, just short and big-breasted and wearing a faded denim button-down. The shiny snaps strain at her chest. "We empty garbage. Vacuuming, we do quarterly. It's the job contract."

"Quarterly?" I look down at the grey-beige carpeting where my knees just were. Then I look at the woman with a wad of black garbage bags ballooning from her pocket. "I was just leaving. Feel free to – " I gesture aimlessly; her gaze does not follow. I have to go behind the door to get my coat from its hook. When I duck back around, one arm already sleeved, she is walking down the hall. Not stomping, just walking.

*

They are mopping the shiny linoleum at the hospital. Even though I tried to shake the rain off myself in the foyer, I still drip with every step. There's always something to feel guilty about. "You look for guilt," my mother would say, if she weren't on oxygen and discouraged from removing her mask to say unnecessary things.

Her bed is in the corner of the wardroom under the window, which she never looks out. I wonder if the other patients resent her for that. I would. Her bed-curtain is pulled shut. Through it, I can make out Desi silhouetted by the flicker-flash of TV. I assume my mother is there too, but in silhouette, she is indistinguishable from a lumpy bed.

"Hey, Mom. Hey, Des." As I slip in, they are watching a big blond man heft a shining grey plank of stone that will become, in the next half hour, a kitchen counter. Like magic.

"Hey, Belinda. Some lady took the other chair." Desi sits slack in the remaining chair. Her hair is loose feathers and random ringlets, sprawled over her shoulders.

"S'ok, I'll sit on the bed." My mother kicks and fidgets towards the window until there is room for me. I sit beside her legs, put a hand on her shin: the bone feels as hard and heavy as ever. She shoves the screen back on its revolving arms so I can see.

*

My mother was diagnosed with cancer when she was already pretty sick, though the coughing and breathlessness seemed worse once we knew they were associated with the big C. She started having to be admitted to the hospital just a couple months later, and now it's been a year of this, of Des and I circling around and hanging out in a sleepy, nearly silent way that is all we can think of since she's been dying. Before this, the three of us never really spent much time together.

It's strange to find I don't mind all the togetherness. We like the same shows, and I've had the PVR for so long, it seems organic to be watching as stuff airs, on the tiny screen attached to my mother's bed. Since I've been spending all my time with work problems or my mom, I've lost track of the PVR – I could have 35 hours of *Top Chef*.

Only a year and I can barely remember what I did every evening when my mother was well and my company wasn't foundering, or at least back when I was ignorant of both issues. I know I subscribed to Netflix, to an organic vegetable delivery program, to eHarmony. I know every couple of weeks I would stride into a Starbucks and look for a man who was looking for me. I know I liked the Netflix better. I wonder what my mother was doing in the evenings, before she was dying.

I leave around 10:30, after prime time is over and my mother is slack under the crunchy white sheets. In the elevator, Des asks me how work is, and I say, "Fine," because it is only a four-storey ride. I always feel I should hug her narrow shoulders before we go to our cars, but there is no history of hugging between us.

*

The next morning, I am congested before I am even conscious. The drenching yesterday has caught up with me. The snot is thin and slippery as blood, without the wet-metal smell. It's tempting to stay in bed, but the customer service reps are not going to lay themselves off, and I can't bear the look my staff gives me when I delegate tasks like this. I use four tissues while getting dressed. I can't face food, so there's nothing left to do but go to work.

The rain has turned to sleet — it clings to me in big icy drops and the wind buffets through my trenchcoat. While I am crossing a patch of ice, the phone buzzes in my pocket and almost knocks me off balance. Once I'm safely in the driver's seat I've missed the call. I dial Desi back without starting the engine. Ice-water drips from my hair onto my neck.

"What's going on?"

"Nothing. I was just thinking you could bring a pizza from that Iranian place tonight. Since it's on your way."

"You were thinking about dinner at eight in the morning?"

"I wanted to get you before work. I know you don't like interruptions."

I can't remember ever saying that, specifically, but it's true. "What do you want on it? Nothing?"

"Is that cool?"

"Sure, nothing's fine. I'll bring it."

"See you tonight."

*

The office is so bright and warm after the slick deluge outside. Wet spots form on the carpet in my office, drips from my coat and hair. The carpet is a grey-brown and you can't really tell if it needs to be vacuumed or not. The wastebasket, however, is most certainly empty.

After I look for the missing HR dossiers for customer service on three drives, I go ask my assistant. The budget is so tight this year, assistants are paid like drive-through staff, and there's not enough of them. Kat's tiny eyebrows scrunch tight as she listens to my request. An hour later, she comes to report that we don't have those employees because their files aren't in our system.

"I'm sure they work here, and if we hired them, there must be files. Files don't prove existence; existence necessitates files."

Kat sags, a pantomime of exhaustion. "I'm sorry, but if we have no files and you don't know their names, how can I search?"

"By category. Just try to think where they would've been classified, if not the right place." I wonder what she wants to be when she grows up. Kat's thick-framed glasses and hair slanting across her forehead look like she's trying hard, but not at HR. "They had paperwork once, it's just gone now. I got the head-count requests when they were hired."

"They could've quit or been let go."

"No, I'm letting them go *now* – I'd remember if I'd done it already." I want to clamp my hands over my mouth, but Kat's job *is* supposed to be dealing with sensitive information. I'm supposed to be training her.

"Really?" Kat straightens. "When's the meeting? Do I need to prepare anything?" Once someone can be laid off, anyone can.

"No – unless you want to go down to the CSR room and take names?"

She lowers her gaze to look through the tiny panels of her glasses directly at me. I guess she is trying to tell if I am kidding. "I don't – I don't know anyone up there."

"Then just see what you can find in the system."

She nods hard. "OK, thanks." Takes a step backwards. "I will."

*

After the last conference call of the day, I rest my forehead on the wrist cushion in front of my keyboard, listening to the hum of the

CPU. The computer doesn't seem to be having any problems today.

The sound of a throat clearing makes me jerk my head up, a ribbon of snot spooling to the desk. The cleaning woman is in the doorway, today in a black *Raiders* shirt. She has a vacuum cleaner.

"You ok?"

I wipe my nose with the back of my hand and it smears across my cheek. "Just resting. You're early?"

"No, on time. We're always on time."

The windows are black and icy; my legs are stiff. I've slept. The watch on my snotty wrist says 7:27. "Yes, you are." On my second try, I stand all the way up. "I'll get out of your way, just let me log out."

I shut applications and log off without even checking email, but as soon as I look up, she says, "I'll vacuum now, but just this once. We are contracted only for quarterly."

The screen goes black. "You don't have – "

"You are exec, I see the doorplate, we can make an exception."

I try to sigh, but the breath won't go in that deeply. I go toward my coat behind the door, but I guess it sort of looks like I'm coming for her.

Backing up, she says, "Or later. We here for an hour." I watch her dragging the vacuum down the hall as I do up my coat. The back of her jersey says Biletnikoff. A Russian name, maybe, or Polish? I think the Raiders play football. But who am I kidding? I will never have a pleasant chat about sports with this woman.

It seems almost impossible now to go up the north stairs to the call centre and look for names I can search in the database. However, if by Monday's update meeting I've accomplished nothing, the executive team will offer only baffled frowns and a desire for outside consultants. I need to figure this out.

But all the call stations are generic – no décor or sweaters, and no nameplates. They must rotate cubes among part-timers. When I open the drawers I see pens and garbage and the occasional pack of gum, nothing identifying. All the computers are shut down, part of an energy-saving policy I myself instituted. I wouldn't know the passwords, anyway.

I'm defeated, but stand there a moment trying to picture this room a few hours ago, warm with bodies and loud with subscription rates, re-orders, misdirected mail. I am sure they are good at their jobs, whoever they are.

*

I stagger through the hospital parking lot with pizza and drinks, no hand free for an umbrella against the sloppy wet snow, and my nose is running. In the fluorescent warmth of the entranceway hangs the sign I've passed a million times, above the hand-cleanser dispenser. There's the usual detailed explanation of how to wash one's hands, and then below, the ban on sick people that always seemed logical until now:

We ask that you do not visit if you have any of the following symptoms:
- Vomiting
- Diarrhea
- Symptoms of acute respiratory tract infection including cough, sore throat, runny nose and/or fever
- Fever within the last 24 hours
- Conjunctivitis (eye infection or pink eye)
- Chicken pox, shingles, measles or mumps
- Infectious rashes or concerns of possible transmission of a communicable disease

If you are suffering from any of these symptoms please see your doctor and/or delay your visit until the symptoms have gone.

I do not have a respiratory tract infection. I have a crust on the inside corners of my eyes and my nose is red from blowing with stiff white toilet paper at work, but my breathing is fine through my mouth. I think of my mother's gritty rasp under her plastic mask, the faint crackle of plastic mattress when I sit on the bed, the cheerful blonde bachelorette on TV, the warmth of my sister's arm and thigh leaning in next to me. A violent sneeze rips through my skull, and I twist my face into my wet sleeve just in time.

Back in the parking lot, my eyes watering, the pizza box still scorches my hands but the rest of me is freezing. I get into the car and dial; Desi picks up on the third ring.

"Where are you? I'm hungry. The nurse said Mom can have pizza, if she feels up to it."

"I have a cold."

"Oh. Sorry. But Mom's got lung cancer, right?" There's some noise in the background – I hope she's laughing. "So go get the pizza and get over here." More muttering. "Mom says actually, just come and we'll order in. They'll deliver to the lobby. I didn't know that."

"I *got* the pizza. I'm here. Well, I'm in the parking lot. But I'm *sick*. Germy?" Sleet drums on the car roof. "Mom's immune system is compromised, not to mention the rest of the people in the hospital. They're not going to let a germy person in."

"You're in the parking lot? With the pizza?"

I tip my head back. There is a lot of lighting out here. Everything gleams bright as day, but spookier. "Yeah, in the purple zone. Can you come down now?"

A thunk and murmuring. "Yeah, just let me put my shoes on."

"I'll flash my lights when – " Click. I tip my head back to face the ceiling, the pizza still hot on my thighs. When we were kids, Desi and I never fought; we just didn't interact at all, slid by each other. In the kitchen reaching for granola bars or in the bathroom reaching for tampons, her arm would be there too, and I would hand her the plastic-wrapped whatever, and she would say thank you, and go back to her room, or outside, or where I didn't know.

She taps on the window, then tries the door and gets in, icewater dripping from her thin blonde hair. She leans over the gearshift and peers at me in the reflected glare. "It's bright but weird out here; I can't really see you. Are you all that sick?"

"Want to risk it? She sounds like a garbage truck idling as it is."

She stares forward. "She's a bit better today."

"Really?"

"Ah, probably not. But she laughed a lot during *Ellen*."

"That's something. And she'll like the pizza."

"Yeah."

"Take it on up to her. You're missing *The Bachelorette*. She can never keep them all straight." I hold up the box, but she doesn't take it, or glance at me.

"I'll go in a second. It's sorta peaceful out here. The rain on the roof is like a white noise machine."

I can feel a sneeze starting in behind my sinuses, and whip my head around before it bursts out. I wipe my nose on the shoulder of my raincoat and I turn back.

"Ok, ok, you are sick."

"I think the pizza's still ok. I mean, it's in the box."

"Sure." She pulls it into her lap, still staring at the wet windshield.

"Are *you* ok?"

"Sure."

"You're here all day every day. Maybe you should take a break."

She shrugs, and the cheap shiny vinyl of her coat makes a crinkling noise against the seat. "What else is a sabbatical for? I'll have to go back to work in the spring."

I think about the spring, when it won't be so dangerous to drive after dark, and that dark will come later, and I'll have to start organizing the interviews for the summer interns, and my mother will probably be dead. "And work is a break?"

"As much as anything, isn't it?"

I shrug. My coat doesn't crinkle. It's cashmere.

She doesn't speak, and when I turn, her face is right in front of mine. "I don't think I should take the germ pizza. I'll order

183

another. Anyway, you need dinner too." She looks at me hard before sliding out of the car. By the time I get home, the pizza is cold.

*

I could simply email the customer service supervisor and ask her the names of her staff. Her name is Suyin Li – that file is where it should be, in the Departmental Supervisors folder. But Kat already hates me, as do the cleaners, my bosses, the orderlies who mop at the hospital, and probably others I don't even know about. In a week or so, when I ask Suyin Li to pass her scripts and quota sheets to the new team in Chennai, she will too, and I'm in no hurry. So I go into the file room. Most people's hire files are kept on paper, too, though the online ones are what's updated.

It is a relief to cough unheard – the filing cabinets don't jerk away or reach for hand santizer, like the people in my meetings this morning. We were listening to staffing requests we can't honour – no $90,000 web designer for *Dream Car,* no consultant fees for the branding team. But I need to take middle management's concerns seriously, make people feel heard, value all stakeholders. And I do, with Kat grudgingly taking notes in the corner – and then I hold up a copy of their departmental budget.

I've always liked this dark, windowless file room. I've worked here too long; I shouldn't be saying *always.* And it's a pretty pathetic thing to love – Kat and her predecessors have left the files jumbled, some shedding pages from being jammed into the cabinet upside-down. But after an hour, I do miraculously find the file of that big black guy because his security badge photo slipped out. He is Wayne LaPorte. He came on a temp contract, but was made full-time. So he'll be owed termination pay. His resume is in the file; we went to the same high school, fifteen years apart.

*

Somewhere outside the file room, five p.m. passes. I just keep searching, because where have I got to go? Eventually I go back to my desk, open the performance evaluation spreadsheets, and enter Wayne LaPorte's employee number. And there's Wayne – his history of service and sick days, his not-quite-excellent performance evaluation, his three 50-cents/hour raises in the last two years. All seems correct except the employment category, which is somehow "Customer" instead of "Customer Service Representative."

I try entering *Customer* in the search category field, and it's the jackpot. All my lost customer service representatives – Danvir, William, Kyla, Susan, half-a-dozen more. All "Customers." Like lost friends found.

There is a rustle, then a bang, then a male voice shouting. He sounds sort of Italian today. I start to stand. I don't want to cause another vacuum-cleaning emergency. Then the phone rings. The real one.

"What's going on?"

"Nothing. I just want you to pick up Booster Juice on the way."

"I'm *sick*. I have a cold. Remember yesterday?" I look at the bin of crumpled Post-its, then look at the doorway. Still clear.

"Are you home?"

"No, still at work."

"I thought you were sick?"

I flop back in my chair. "I have a cold that makes me too germy for the hospital. I'm not dying or anything."

We're both silent for a moment, probably both thinking about how inappropriate that was. The cleaning woman comes in just as Desi says, "She liked having us both here, watching TV, eating supper. It was like we're little kids after school."

"I don't – " I think about whether it's all right to complain about your childhood when your mother is dying. I see the waste-basket rising silently beside me. The cleaning-woman's full-time job used to be my Saturday morning chore. "I don't remember all that many warm after-school chats. Didn't we mainly watch *Golden Girls* reruns and eat marshmallows while we waited for her to come home from work?"

"Sometimes *WKRP in Cinncinnati*. And sometimes she'd make proper snacks."

"And those were good shows, anyway."

"Right. It's not like we had miserable childhoods."

"I never thought that. I never thought much about it at all. Are you in the hall?"

"Of course. What kind of daughter do you think I am?"

"What kind of daughter do you think *I* am, Desi? I'd be there if I could."

There is a pause. "What are you working on?"

A longer pause. At least the cleaner has gone into the hall now. "Layoffs."

"Seriously? A lot?"

"I said I was a good daughter, not a good VP."

"If it makes you feel any better, I'm not a good prof."

"You probably are. You were a good babysitter. It's the same skill set, right?"

"Yeah, basically. But I was never that good. You were just young."

"So were you."

"Sorry, Belinda. I should go back."

"Well. Tell her I said hi."

"Ok. Good night. Feel better."

I am staggering down the hallway in my coat when the cleaning lady comes out of an office carrying another wastebin. She screams something down the hall the other way, at no one I can see, then dumps the garbage in her cart.

My breath is a snotty wheeze, loud enough that she looks up from the Coke cans and apple cores. "Yes? Another problem?"

I didn't even realize our relationship was like this now: the frown lines, the wastebin frozen in mid-air, the gaze darting in search for her invisible colleague: resignation, but also rage.

"No, no problem."

She stares at me – I have to walk away for this to be over. So I do. I call over my shoulder, "No problem at all. You're doing a fine job." She is still staring.

After the bend in the hallway, I lean against the wall, feeling short of breath. I tip my head back, inhale, and when I level my gaze, Kat is staring at me. Her cube being in the hall is a building services decision that I don't even try to parse, but she's there amidst her posters of bands I don't recognize and pictures of kittens. She takes out one earbud, then the other – a show of respect.

"You should go, Kat – it's pretty late. Whatever it is will wait."

She pokes her skinny fingers under her glasses and rubs her eyes, hard. "I can't find them. I don't know how they could possibly be filed, I can't work it out."

"The customer service reps?"

Kat yanks her hands down, maybe scared that there's something else to look for. "You asked me to find them."

She's wearing a sharp-collared, bright orange blouse, a heavy silver necklace, smokey eyeshadow. All this to look pretty – she's so pretty – and the only person she sees all day is me, for 90 seconds. And then she has to go back to her cube in the hallway.

"I found them, just now. They were misfiled under *Customer*, for some reason."

I smile but Kat doesn't, and her thin orange shoulders do not relax. "Misfiled?"

How can I be intimidating when my mascara is smeared by sneeze-tears? "Weird, eh?"

Her shoulders wriggle. "Yeah, it is. I don't know how – "

"Go home, Kat. Tomorrow, something else will go wrong."

She goes almost limp with relief, and reaches immediately for the small leather pouch hanging on the wall beside her. "Thanks,

Belinda. Really, thanks for helping me. Maybe tonight will be good after all." She gives me a brief open-mouthed grin. She must reserve it for silly friends, puppies, flirtatious waiters – I've never seen it before.

*

In high school, people called me *the pretty one* and Des *the smart one,* even though my grades were decent and she looked better in a miniskirt. And now we are both zooming past 40, and both powerfully employed and single, and I imagine we are unlikeable in more similar ways now. At least, I think she's still single – she could have fallen in love with a fellow chemist or my mom's nurse, and I wouldn't have known.

On the highway, the flare of brake lights reflects off the slush. I am bleary, tired, and scared a strong sudden sneeze will shut my eyes and jerk my hands from the wheel. It would be so awkward at work if I died: I am a VP. They would have to have a memorial for me in the large conference room, with urns of coffee and a PowerPoint presentation with photos of me wearing a crooked Santa hat in front of a pile of toy-drive presents. The night cleaners would not be invited.

At Islington, I realize it's Friday. Friday, a TV dead zone when even those who fail to have plans would at least rent a DVD, or PVR something, or sedate themselves. It is Friday night, I have a wheeze in my throat, maybe some old eps of *Top Chef,* and I *can not remember* whether the marshmallows my mother gave my sister and I when she had to work late were coloured or plain, or, for that matter, which I preferred. Why didn't I savour my childhood more, so that now, when for the next 60 hours no one expects me anywhere, I could have something sweet to look back on?

I turn off Rexdale onto Martingrove and finally sneeze when I'm at the lights, waiting for green, waiting to be at Etobicoke General, the only place I want to be. The snot courses onto my upper lip and into my mouth, but someone beeps – green – so I can't find a Kleenex until I am parked, idling so the heat can stay on, rummaging in my purse, gazing up at the warm safe lights of the dying.

I am comfortable here. This car is expensive, well-cushioned, and fully paid off. I am the only one to have driven it, with almost no passengers, besides my mother on the way to doctors' appointments. Perhaps she dropped something in beside the seat – a barrette or receipt. If I find it after she is dead, will it be a tender moment or a creepy one? I could probably use more to remember her by. I think I would be happy if I found her barrette.

I sneeze into my shoulder even though there is no one there. I count the lighted windows of the hospital, trying to figure out which one is my mom's, if I'm even on the right side. As long as I sit here, I will be nearby and accessible when the final call comes. I realize that I am a stalker of death. Maybe I am bad luck. I have my phone in my hand and am speed-dialing before I can think about it anymore.

"Hey, Des, how is she?"

"Fine. She was tired tonight, actually. She fell asleep."

"She could use the rest." I flop back so the snot won't ooze down my face.

"Did you wind up going home?"

"I'm on my way now." This is nearly true. An ambulance flashes loud and red into the lot. If Des hears it both through my phone and in her world, she doesn't say.

"Maybe I'll head back to mom's place and sleep, too. May as well."

"Did you eat? You could come by mine, if she's out for the night? We could eat something . . . You'd have to stay well away from my germs, of course."

A low chuckle. I can't think of the last time she was in my house, or I even wanted her to be. "Belinda, that's nice of you, but is there anything in your fridge?"

"We'd have to order in," I admit.

"Well . . . fine. I'm just gonna go check on her, and then I'll – Oh, shit, it's snowing again."

The wet flakes are splattering my windshield. "I can pick you up, so you don't have to drive. It's practically on my way. I can bring you back to your car tonight, or even in the morning."

"Oh, Belle, you don't have to. I'll be fine."

"It's no trouble, Des, none – I'm really close right now, so it'd be easy. Where I am right now, I'm so close."

Acknowledgements

Several of these stories have appeared previously in journals and anthologies, some in slightly different forms. I wish to thank the editors of *Canadian Notes & Queries, Hart House Review, Room, Prairie Fire, The Fiddlehead,* and *Best Canadian Short Stories* for their support and guidance.

I'd also like to thank my fellow writers who read these stories early and late, and told me what they really thought: Kerry Clare, Brahm Nathans, Nadia Pestrak, Mark Sampson, and S. Kennedy Sobol. Gratitude to Frédérique Delaprée for offering the inspiration behind "Dream Big" and by extension the whole collection. Thanks to Jessica Grant, for whom "How to Keep Your Day Job" was originally written as a performance piece, and to Penny McDougall for the good idea that sparked "Research." And thanks to all my delightful friends for good company (especially the members of Proofville, Lunch Club, and the Women's Writing Salon).

Thanks to everyone who participated in the "professional interviews" on rebeccarosenblum.com – Ben, Fred, Jamie, Jennifer, Kimberly, Martha, Mary, and Scott. While I did not "use" these in the book, your insights truly illuminated my writing.

I'm grateful to my agent, Samantha Haywood, for her astute reading and warm support. It goes without saying (but I will anyway) that I am so lucky to be working with Dan Wells, Tara Murphy, and everyone on team Biblioasis, and that it is always a pleasure. And of course, sincerest thanks go to my editor, the wonderful John Metcalf, for time, insight, interest, and intelligence. Also books. And humour.

Always and forever, thanks to Barbara, Gerald, and Ben Rosenblum, for being my family. And to Mark, for everything.

ABOUT THE AUTHOR

Rebecca Rosenblum's fiction has been short-listed for the Journey Prize, the National Magazine Award, and the Danuta Gleed Award, and she was herself a juror for the Journey Prize 21. Her first collection of short stories, *Once*, won the Metcalf-Rooke Award and was one of *Quill & Quire*'s 15 Books That Mattered in 2008. Her first chapbook, *Road Trips*, was published by Frog Hollow Press in 2010. Her blog is www.rebeccarosenblum.com. Rebecca lives, works, and writes in Toronto, Ontario.